THE BELIEVERS

STORIES

THE
BELIEVERS

STORIES

A. K. HERMAN

A. R. Phillips Press LLC
New York

"Love" was first published in 2023 in *Black Warrior Review.*
"Dark" was first published in 2023 in *Doek! Literary Journal.*
"Exile" was first published in 2022 in the *Coachella Review.*
"Ready for the Revolution?" was first published in 2022 in *Isele Magazine.*
"Believers" was first published in 2022 in *Lolwe.*
"Drink the Dew" was first published in 2021 in *Doek! Literary Journal.*
"Inside" was first published under the title "You Can Always Tell" in *Asteri(x) Journal* in 2016.
"The Iridescent Blue-Black Boy with Wings (After Márquez)" was the second-place winner of the Small Axe Literary Prize in 2012.
"Love Story No. 8: Jane and Phillip" was shortlisted for the Commonwealth short story prize in 2009.

Manufactured in the United States

Library of Congress Control Number: 2024936560

Names: Herman, A. K., 1971– author
Title: The Believers: Stories / A. K. Herman
Description: First edition. | New York: A. R. Phillips Press LLC, 2024
Identifiers: LCCN 2024936560 (print and ebook)
Subjects: LCSH: Short Stories—Fiction | Caribbean immigrants—Fiction | Trinidad and Tobago—Fiction | Interpersonal relations—Fiction | BISAC: FICTION / Short Stories (single author). FICTION / Literary. FICTION / Own Voices

Paperback ISBN: 978-1-948788-01-4

eBook ISBN: 978-1-948788-00-7

A. R. Phillips Press LLC
271 Cadman Plaza E
Unit 21936
Brooklyn, NY 11202
www.arphillipspress.com

THE BELIEVERS

STORIES

A. K. HERMAN

A. R. Phillips Press LLC
New York

"Love" was first published in 2023 in *Black Warrior Review*.
"Dark" was first published in 2023 in *Doek! Literary Journal*.
"Exile" was first published in 2022 in the *Coachella Review*.
"Ready for the Revolution?" was first published in 2022 in *Isele Magazine*.
"Believers" was first published in 2022 in *Lolwe*.
"Drink the Dew" was first published in 2021 in *Doek! Literary Journal*.
"Inside" was first published under the title "You Can Always Tell" in *Asteri(x) Journal* in 2016.
"The Iridescent Blue-Black Boy with Wings (After Márquez)" was the second-place winner of the Small Axe Literary Prize in 2012.
"Love Story No. 8: Jane and Phillip" was shortlisted for the Commonwealth short story prize in 2009.

Manufactured in the United States

Library of Congress Control Number: 2024936560

Names: Herman, A. K., 1971– author
Title: The Believers: Stories / A. K. Herman
Description: First edition. | New York: A. R. Phillips Press LLC, 2024
Identifiers: LCCN 2024936560 (print and ebook)
Subjects: LCSH: Short Stories—Fiction | Caribbean immigrants—Fiction | Trinidad and Tobago—Fiction | Interpersonal relations—Fiction | BISAC: FICTION / Short Stories (single author). FICTION / Literary. FICTION / Own Voices

Paperback ISBN: 978-1-948788-01-4

eBook ISBN: 978-1-948788-00-7

A. R. Phillips Press LLC
271 Cadman Plaza E
Unit 21936
Brooklyn, NY 11202
www.arphillipspress.com

To Almighty God and the Saints.

To Auldith and Kathleen.

Table of Contents

The Dancer is Not a Dancer

Approach this collection like you're walking up to a Caribbean limbo troupe in frilly costumes to pluck a red hibiscus from behind a dancer's ear to discover that the flower is rooted in the skin, and the dancer isn't a dancer at all.

The stories I heard growing up about Tobago, and the lives I witnessed while I lived in Little Caribbean—an area of Brooklyn located on the corridors of Flatbush, Church, Nostrand, and Utica Avenues—are a far cry from the popular trope of island people smiling and dancing in off-the-shoulder flowery garb. What lurks within that flower cupped by a perfect brown ear? Beautiful, rural Tobagonian women who own property and discard lovers, predatory pastors, supernatural creatures that play with children and more.

This collection honors the long tradition of Caribbean and African literature as it retells, echoes and rides the currents of Wilson Harris, Naipaul, and Achebe. The love stories, and the lovers you'll meet, turn nineteenth-century creole romance on its overly coiffed head. In these stories, people talk, think, and do things that you wouldn't otherwise witness unless you were family, a friend, or a lover. No one conforms to type.

A. K. Herman

THE
BELIEVERS
STORIES

"This new boss in work, he don't want to give me any overtime. He want me to pay him in kind for a lil' bit a money. I tell you, if I wasn't a good Christian woman, I call my family in Moruga and, in three days, I get all the overtime I want and he go have he own business to mind."

— SISTER LEWIS, 2011

The Believers

ON AN UNUSUALLY warm September day, Ronald was on Fulton Street, across from Star Botanica Inc.: Religious Items, Candles, Incense, etc. He ate a beef patty and scanned the faces of people passing by for any sign of familiarity. He ate slowly to calm his nerves. He should have gone to the Bronx like his wife, Marva, had suggested. In the Bronx, he was less likely to meet anyone from church, but he didn't know which Botanica in the Bronx had La Pastora. He didn't know if the spirit work was any good, and there was no one he could ask. There was a lull in the parade of buses and livery cabs on Fulton, so he dusted off the orange pastry flakes on his jeans and sprinted across the street.

Just before he went in, he looked for La Pastora among the figures that stood and sat in the store window display. The last time he was at Star, she was at the front in white robes; her kind, porcelain face looked out at him, and her arms were held wide as if she was about to embrace a person who had not yet arrived. But now, La Pastora was tucked in a corner behind Xhango, who was striking a Hulk pose in red cutoff pants. A yellow-haired deity in a blue cape and relief gold jewelry on his chest brandished a sword that blocked La Pastora's face—goddess upstaged.

Ping, ping! The bell hit the glass door when he opened it.

Inside, the store looked different. The bare wooden counter was still there, but opposite the counter were shelves from the floor to just above Ronald's head. The eye-level shelves were crowded with red and pink candles shaped like vaginas, penises, and humans. Below those were candles in glass containers: bright yellow, white, black, red, green, and blue. Under those were foil-wrapped incense sticks and dark bottles with the names of the oils they contained written in black marker on white masking tape. Ronald took some sage incense sticks from the shelf and walked to the back of the line of customers that ran along the counter. When it was his turn, the girl leaned her shaved head to one side and asked, "What you need help with today?"

"Mi want to burn two light. One to pass mi exam-dem. One fi mi wife pass her exam and she finish school."

"That's it? Anything for money, work or you see somebody you want?" The girl smiled. She was probably as old as his daughter, Shereen, and Ronald fought the urge to ask why she wasn't in school.

"Nah, just di exam-dem and school. And mi want to burn di light-dem wid Pastora. You still work wid her?"

"Yes, we work with all the good saints." She took two yellow candles from the shelf behind her, put them on the counter and brushed each one with a paintbrush dipped in oil. She clasped both candles, closed her eyes, then murmured something Ronald couldn't hear. When she opened her eyes, she threw silver glitter from a rusted metal can on each candle then gave Ronald two small white envelopes. "Parchment. Write your desire on this. Your wife too. Put the parchment under each candle and let them burn without stopping. It should burn in front of La Pastora. You have a picture? Nine-fifty for the small one and fifteen for the big one." She reached across the counter and tapped the front of the glass case with one finger.

"No, mi have dat."

"You know how to write the desire…what you want? We have a book that tell you how. Four ninety-five."

"Mi know how. How much?"

"You know Father Cuffy here today, right? He is the best seer man in Brooklyn right now. Everything he say come to pass. I could keep the candles here while you wait to see him."

"Not today." He searched his mind to see if the urge was strong, to see if La Pastora wanted him to see Cuffy. "No, next time. How much fi ebriting?"

"Thirty for the two candles. Three each for the parchment. Thirty-six."

He held up the incense so she could see it.

"Plus three. Thirty-nine altogether."

He gave her the cash.

Ping! The bell chimed as he left the store.

◈

Leaves reddened in October, and a cold wind whipped up dust and paper. Ronald closed his eyes, leaned against the black wrought-iron gate that separated the New Community Church from the outside world, and raised the collar of his coat to cover his nape. The women's group was bubbling out the wooden front door, all pastel hats and dark wool coats. At the end of the parade of hats, he saw his daughter, Shereen. She lingered near the door with Harold, head of the youth group, and Jacqueline, a thin girl who looked on at the other two, mirroring their actions like a shadow. Shereen was laughing at something Harold said. Harold had both hands in his pockets and a tug in his impeccable cheek exposed a dimple. Each time his lips moved, Shereen covered her heart-shaped mouth with her hands and laughed. The other girl smiled whenever Shereen laughed. Ronald thought that his daughter was laughing too loudly, and was walking toward the door to give her a look when he felt a hand on his back. He turned.

"Brother Davis!" The voice filled Ronald's head.

"Pastor Columbus." Ronald grasped the grayish knobby root held out to him. "Sermon strong today, Boss."

"Thank you, Brother. The sermon is not mine. Is the Lord's. 'Cause…" He paused then exclaimed, "Jesus said, Speak!" He bent his knees and straightened up again. "Speak! And I will putteth words in thine mouth. Eh heh." The root gripped Ronald's hand.

"Amen," the people mumbled. "Praise Jesus."

Out of the corner of one eye, Ronald saw Marva weave between the church people and head toward the wrought-iron gate. He hoped that Marva had collected Anthony, their ten-year-old son, and was ready to go.

"Praise di Lawd," Ronald said. The people corralled behind the gate seemed to be holding their breaths.

"Now, Brother. I want to talk to you about a personal matter." Columbus touched his shoulder and, for the first time, Ronald noticed the pastor wasn't wearing a coat. His bright orange shirt and gold brocade waistcoat were brilliant in the reddish light.

Ronald touched the shorter man's shoulder with his other hand so they looked like they were in a distant embrace.

"A delicate matter." Columbus smiled, showing perfect dentures. "A matter to be discussed among men."

Conversations had started up again, but a few brothers stood with their backs to the main conversation. Ronald sensed tension in these men. The back seams of their coats were wires pulled tight.

"You know that God know what is best for His children, eh. You agree?"

Ronald nodded.

"And sometimes God make a choice for we that we don't know we need. Eh heh, Brother?" Columbus's eyes, laced with red veins, searched Ronald's. "You agree, Brother?"

Ronald nodded again so the pastor would continue.

"Now." Columbus tiptoed and leaned in as if he was about to kiss him. "God has blessed you with a beautiful daughter, a daughter who is about to become a woman…"

Ronald lowered his coat collar and made a line in his brow so he could look like he was thinking, listening hard.

"…and the Bible say, for women to remain godly, they should cleave to a man of God. And through this man, the woman would find communion with God lest she be lost from the flock. You see what I saying, eh?" Columbus brought his lips to Ronald's ear. "It only a matter a time before Shereen tempt the youth leader to fornication. Let we do right in the eyes of God and marry them in the church so she might find God through him and continue to live in righteousness."

"Mi…mi go have to tek a rain check on dat and get back to you." Ronald smiled and stepped back, the pastor still holding his hand.

Columbus clasped the handshake with his other hand and stepped back too. "Okay, you going get back to me. You talk like them Americans now, eh! You go take a rain check, eh? But don't wait too long."

"Look like Miss Cleo want talk to you, Boss." Ronald smiled at the pastor's wife.

Columbus let go of Ronald and turned to face her. "Oh yes. My dear."

"Fletcher, we have distribution in half hour and we want you bless the food." Cleopatra's pale-blue *Starship Enterprise* of a hat bobbed above her broad face. She smiled at Ronald and her silver front tooth looked black in the blue umbra of the hat.

"Right, right." Columbus looked at his watch. "Is already one."

Cleopatra draped an arm around her husband and led him away.

Ronald felt like he was swaying and went through the open gate. Marva, Shereen, and Anthony waited on the other side.

When they turned the corner at 35th Street and Church Avenue, Marva asked, "What him want?"

"Ebriting," Ronald said.

❧

Ronald blew into his cup of hot Ovaltine. The steam settled on the window and obscured his view of the street. He lifted his finger to write something in the brief, white fog that had settled on the glass then dropped it to his side and turned around to find Marva standing at the kitchen door.

"Early morning you worrying? Drinking tea and looking out?" She smiled and put one arm around him.

"Mi want mi own house."

"But we get a house." She gestured at the ceiling and walls.

"Dis di church people—dem house. Church is co-signer. Fletcher and Cleopatra have di paper—dem too. So, is really dem house."

"We didn't have credit for mortgage. What you saying? If they didn't help we—"

"Marv, mi don't think dem really help we. Mi thinking now…dat…dat we coulda do it fi we self. Mi going tell you something." He looked out the window at a tall broad-shouldered woman in a black coat over white scrubs and white plastic shoes with holes that showed bright pink socks. The woman reminded him of his mother, a grand woman who cleaned houses for a living and sent him to school under the threat of death if he didn't attend. Ronald faced Marva. "Is frighten mi did frighten, why mi did ask Fletcher to co-sign on di house. Frighten 'bout di great Amerika and credit and things mi didn't understand. Frighten and grateful 'cause dem help we find work and…get papers and"—he put the cup on the windowsill and pulled her near him—"and after all dat, mi still frighten to go out on mi own in di big Amerika. Mi get papers but mi still feel somebody going ketch mi." He grabbed the air just in front of his face with one hand, held it in a tight fist, and pressed the fist on the glass. "Look at me. Big man like me 'fraid to buy him own house?"

"We can transfer the house to we."

"Is pass papers now. We live three blocks from di church. Attend service ebri Sunday. We in coat drive. Food drive. Orphan drive. Bumboclaat drive! We lock in. And now...now dem want mi daughter." When he first migrated, Ronald fought to change his speech to match Marva's more refined patois and because he didn't want to announce to everyone he met that he was from the wrong side of Kingston. Now, patois soothed him, like a well-loved meal. His mother's Jamaican patois on the phone was like blue jays in the morning—sharp, noisome music.

"Ronnie, I talk to Shereen awready. I tell she to have little to do with Harold. Jus' hello and thank you. I tell Tony not to talk 'bout things that happen in the house. If they ask you any question, tell them to ask me or you daddy."

"Look at we. Something wrong. You go to college under di cover a darkness. Mi did study accounting at Mona and now mi putting up drywall and tekin' insult from dem-Italians-dem. Mi tekin' CPA classes. And we can't tell nobody in church? Marv," he whispered, "We burnin' light to make things go good fi we." Then raised his voice again. "If dat is di case, we not in any church." He sucked his teeth, the sound like paper tearing. "We...we...mi don't know. But we have to get out. 'Cause dem own we. And now Fletcher want married Shereen to dat...dat bwoy. And him ask me in di churchyard, where ebribody can hear. He...what dem Amerikan say? When you do something wicked, but you do it nice-nice. People know you doing wick-edness, but you so nice-nice that somebody going look crazy to get wrathed wid you?"

"Passive aggressive." She scraped a spot off the window with the nail of one thumb.

"Yes. We have to be passive aggressive too. Underneath." He folded his arms across his chest.

Marva moved so she faced him. "I could ask Cleopatra. I could ask she where we paper is. And we could talk to the bank or to a real estate agent to tell we how to get the co-borrower off the house."

"Dem have some places on Nostrand Avenue. You could check—"

"No Ronnie. No place 'round here. We have to stop thinking so. We have to get advice from someplace else, like in Manhattan. Or you know what? We should talk to people. You talk to the man-dem in work and I go ask people in school and in work. They can recommend somebody good, somebody they work with awready."

"You correct. But Fletcher get di jobs fi we. Boss man know di people-dem. Him might know staff in di nursing home too."

"He say so, but I there three years, and nobody never call he name or he wife name to me. I think he just send we there and we get things on we own luck. You ever hear he name mention? If he and Vincent and Glen was fren-fren, he woulda be there sometime or they woulda talk 'bout him."

"Awright. You have a point. We should feel di

people out first before we ask dem. You never know who people is till you know who people is. You feel out Cleopatra."

"I go do that. You still worrying?" She touched his forehead.

He wrinkled his forehead so that more crooked lines formed under her fingertips. "Mi didn't married to you for you shine eye alone, you know."

"Mek you married to me for, Mr. Davis?"

Ronald leaned to one side until he could look behind her, and pointed at her bottom with his bottom lip. "Mi did see a bumpa walking 'round by Miss Joyce and mi did say, mi going married dat bumpa." He slapped her hard on the buttocks. "First chance mi get," he shouted.

She laughed and hugged him. He rocked her from side to side; his erection fingered her stomach.

"Daddy, we not going to church today?" a voice asked.

Ronald stopped moving and saw that Shereen spanned the doorway with both arms. "Yes."

Anthony, looking gift-wrapped in green dinosaur pajamas, shot under Shereen's armpit and hugged both his parents.

"We getting ready or we having a family hug?" Shereen shrugged and rolled her eyes.

"We going. You and you brother go bathe. Start to get ready." He looked down at Anthony. "Go wid you sister."

"But, Daddy…you and Mame come to bathe too."

"Go." Ronald flicked his chin toward the doorway that Shereen had already left vacant.

The boy went.

"Bathe and dress," Marva yelled, then put one hand over a giggle.

"Yeah, bathe. Mi and you mother soon come," Ronald added. They held hands as they went up the stairs to their bedroom and locked the door.

⁓

According to the written program, the service was supposed to be over after the last hymn. Ronald looked up at the LCD screen above the sanctuary and mouthed the words to the last verse of *How Great Thou Art* that kept repeating across the screen. Pastor Columbus, in a burgundy suit with matching satin waistcoat, was next to the pulpit with the mic in one hand. A woman screamed from the front pew and Ronald tiptoed to see who it was.

"Hallelujah," the Screamer shouted and walked until she was in the middle aisle, facing the congregation. The Screamer looked like a thin puppet in a shapeless gray jacket and skirt that reached almost to her ankles.

"Bangee-muhnah-canophanee…" The Screamer shouted and started spinning around and bending at the waist as if she was trying to fling her torso into the congregation. Ronald touched Marva with his elbow, but didn't look at her. "Sister Lewis turn to ketch it," he whispered.

across from him. Anthony and Sister Lewis completed the circle. He and his family closed their eyes and repeated the prayer Sister Lewis recited.

When the prayer was over, Navy Hat began, "I see things going well for you and your family. There was many stumbling blocks in the past...'bout money... hmmm...'bout family life, but you overcome that. You, Brother Davis, had a curse on you. From your father side. I can't see who do it, but that in the past now." She narrowed her eyes to peer into Ronald's. "But I see hardship in the future. Troubles. Not sure the source... I see a woman...youngish. Can't see she face. Don't know if she the source of trouble or if she is the one who will see trouble."

"A-hep!" Cleopatra got on her tiptoes, yanked Ronald's arm toward her then planted her feet on the floor. When he glanced at her, she squeezed his hand. "Things hidden will reveal. Secrets will come out. Watch and pray, Brother and Sister Davis. A-hep! Troubles ahead...sssssssssss..."

In the background, Columbus was on the mic. "Hymn number thirty-four. *Blessed Assurance*."

The congregation sang, "Blessed assurance, Jesus..."

"Let us pray," Cleopatra began. "Heavenly Father, whom in thine..."

After the prayer, the family returned to their seats to listen to the pastor's message. During the singing of the benediction, Ronald wrote a note on his program and showed it to Marva: *Home now. No meeting.*

Marva put on her coat without looking at him, helped Anthony with his coat, then held her son at the shoulders. Ronald whispered to Shereen, "We walking straight out di gate. Put on you coat."

"But youth group, Daddy?"

"Mi nah a play, chile!" His eyes felt hot.

Shereen's eyes widened for a moment then she put on her coat.

Once the benediction ended, the stewards walked to the back and opened the varnished doors.

Ronald placed the palm of one hand on the inlet of Marva's back and felt her body stiffen. The moment the man who drove the church van got up, she headed straight for the door. Ronald followed her and the children, the murmur of the church behind him.

∽

They missed two Sundays in a row. Sister Lewis called on the afternoon of the first Sunday and Marva lied that Anthony had brought home the flu. On the second Sunday, Ronald answered the phone. Cleopatra called to say that she had added their names to the roster of the Healing Group so that the group could make a prayer visit. Ronald leaned against the fridge as he talked. He watched Marva's shoulders drop when he said the family was fine and would return to church the following Sunday.

"Yes, yes. Mi can do dat. Saturday evening. No problem." He paused. "Same to you and God bless,

Sister." He hung up, squatted near the ground, and put his face in his hands. The darkness and the skin smell made him feel like he was somewhere else. He pressed his hands into his eyes until red swirls formed in the darkness.

"What you going do for them next Saturday?" Marva's voice was high-pitched.

Ronald uncovered his eyes and stood up. He felt giddy and the light was too bright. "Dem want me help drywall di church basement."

She shrugged and went back to the dishes.

"What you did want me to say? Eh, Marv? Dem want to bring di prayer group."

From the back, her shoulders looked square under the frayed cream sweater. Her bright-colored head tie made her head look small.

"Marv?"

"It don't matter now, Ronald Davis. You say yes awready. But you didn't ask what I think 'bout it first."

Water hit the dishes in the sink and he opened his mouth to say something, then closed it and went back to the books spread across the living room table.

❧

During the break, Ronald sat on a bucket of joint compound and the other two men, Felix and Winston, sat on plastic lawn chairs across from him. Felix was talking about how the church had changed his life.

"...to call me Dragon because people used to fraid

me," Felix, the new member from Trinidad, said. "Now, look at me? Working in a place with a roof, not out on the corner selling coke and baking soda."

"You used to mix it with soda?" Winston asked.

Felix shrugged. "Well, yeah! How else yuh go make a living selling powder? Yuh need to give them pipers a piece of a high so they go come back for the nex' piece."

The three men laughed.

Ronald watched Winston's jowl tremble. The scar across Felix's bony cheek danced. It was men like Felix that made him and his wife leave Jamaica. Outlaws in gold-rimmed shades with scars across their necks and missing fingers, who ruled over entire villages and fired at the police for kicks. He used to be afraid that a bullet might pierce his head if he stood near the front window of his mother's house.

"So dis church, Columbus, help you fi real?" Ronald asked.

"Way I see it." Felix turned off his laughter. "Is God who help me. The church is just the means to a end. Yuh understand? Is like smokin' a pipe to get a high." He gathered the first three fingers on one hand as if holding a pipe to his lips. "The pipe don't get yuh high, is the thing inside it. But yuh need the pipe and the fire to burn the thing that does make yuh reach high up. Yuh understand?"

Winston nodded his meaty head and shifted on the chair. It creaked.

"You want exchange?" Ronald pointed at the joint compound bucket.

"Yeah, oh gosh, this chair can't take my weight." Winston said and they exchanged seats.

"Columbus—" Felix stopped for a moment as if listening. "Columbus like them gangstas, dangerous men from Trinidad East-West Corridor, who could get people to do things they don't want to do. 'Cause Columbus understand that, if yuh know what a man want, yuh could own him. A food. A fuck. A money. A house. A car. Once that man take the thing he wanted from yuh hand, yuh could pet him like a dog and he go lick yuh hand. Then, when yuh ready, beat him like a dog too and he go convince he self that yuh do something for he that he couldn't do for he self." Felix stood up and stretched.

Ronald too had seen the Columbus that Felix described and wondered if Felix had more to say. "Wha' island Boss come from?" Ronald asked, as Columbus, over the years, had referred to various islands in the Caribbean. His speech betrayed no particular creole or pidgin. And he never, as far as Ronald knew, talked of a better-than-here paradise that most newcomers imagined home to be, once on foreign soil.

"He from all about, man. He live all about," Felix said.

"And Miss Cleo?" Ronald added quickly, like an empty glass on an already-full tray.

"She is a retired ho from Venezuela." Felix walked over to the wall they had been working on and put his hands on his hips.

A. K. Herman

"Mek you say so?" Ronald kept his eyes on Felix.

"'Cause I know woman like she. Used to have them by the two and three when I used to run business through Margarita Island. If yuh listen good, yuh go hear the Spanish underneath she proper talk." He turned around. "Don't look at me so, Winston. You don't like what I saying about yuh pastor and he wife?"

"No. I—" Winston began.

"Look, what I say don't change nothing. I saying it as I see it. And, like I say, God help me through Columbus and the church. That is why I here on a Saturday working for free." He stretched both arms toward the ceiling and his T-shirt lifted at the back. There were two long, blond scars across his waist and, above them, clusters of shiny raised skin indicated there were more on his upper back.

"Let we finish. Is just two wall. Mi don't want stay till late." Ronald stood.

Winston opened the joint compound bucket. They took the floats from the sink and started again.

Later that evening, as they were cleaning up, Columbus called hello then descended the staircase. "Evening, Brothers," he said when he entered the basement.

Felix was at the sink and tapped elbows with Columbus.

"Evening, Pastor." Winston shook Columbus's hand.

"Thank you for doing this, eh. We just had a

20

meeting and the church elders, Brother Phillip and all the rest, waiting upstairs to thank all of you before you go."

"You're welcome. Is nothing," Winston said.

Ronald turned from packing away his tools and shook Columbus's outstretched hand.

"Thank you, Brother Davis," Columbus said.

"No problem. No problem."

Columbus held on to Ronald's hand, led him to one corner of the room, and leaned in. "How is the family?"

"Ebriting good. Ebribody good."

"And the young lady? You ready to get back to me?"

"We was busy and ebribody did sick. No time to really discuss it wid Marva."

"Hmmm. Your wife help you with decisions, eh. My wife too. You know, my wife told me that Mrs. Davis asked about transferring the title of the house to you and about taking us off."

"Okay." Ronald's heart beat fast.

"This is something we always wanted to do. But church business does keep me so busy that these things slip through the crease. I will do it as soon...in fact, I will do it next week." He sighed. "And I ask your forgiveness for not doing it sooner." He touched Ronald on his shoulder with the other hand. "Do you forgive me, Brother?" His eyes drooped at the sides.

Ronald could feel Winston's eyes on him, so he smiled. "No problem, Boss. Life like dat, you know."

"Good, good. I am so lucky to have you as a friend and as a brother."

The other men started up the steps.

"Good night," Felix yelled from upstairs.

"Wait, mi go walk out wid you," Ronald called after Winston.

At the top of the stairs, Felix was already gone. Ronald shook the hands of church elders held out to him and made sure that with each step he headed for the side door.

⁂

Marva gathered her skirt in her lap, stooped near the floor, and leaned the green candle until three drops of wax had marked the center of the white enamel basin. She stuck a square of parchment to the wax then made the candle bow again, and spilled wax onto the parchment to form a pale green glob, like phlegm on snow. She pressed the base of the candle into the glob and held it there. "Bring some water," she said without looking up.

Ronald heard her but found that he couldn't move. A thought percolated inside him. Its tiny bubbles filled his chest, forced their way up his neck then out his mouth. "Marva, mi nuh think we should do it," he whispered.

"You getting the water or I need to do that for miself too?" She hadn't yet washed her face, and there was a whitish thing at the tails of her eyes.

"Marv. We getting di things we want. But to interfere wid people? Mi always say mi go never do dat."

She stood and faced him. "We not getting everything we want. We want Shereen to make she own decision 'bout who she want to marry and when. We want to go church when we want. We want the house on we name. Is been three months since he say he go change it, and him nah do it yet! We not interfering with them. We just want them to do what we ask." When he didn't answer, she continued, "I know you think this is obeah, but is not. Is the same thing we doing all along. We asking for a favor. As the candle get soft and melt, so them get soft and melt. No harm. No foul. Ronnie?"

"Yeah."

"You see what I saying? If we don't do this, these people going to own we till we dead!"

The candle flickered and made a hissing sound. They both turned to face it.

"See, the candle talking awready." Marva went closer.

Ronald filled the basin and placed it near the wall with the picture of La Pastora.

"I go feel more comfortable if we rest it in the hall bathroom and full the tub," Marva said. "Them things does flare up." The flame doubled in size and the candle hissed. "Lawd!" She took a step back.

"Di kids-dem use dat bathroom. We go have to lock it and Tony wouldn't want to use di downstairs bathroom in di night." He thought for a moment. "Put di basin in a bigger basin of water. We have one in di basement. I go wake dem kids to go school and get di basin."

In the corridor, Ronald heard beeps coming from his daughter's room and knocked on her door.

"Yeah," Shereen answered.

"Mi can open?"

"Yeah, Daddy."

She sat with the gray covers over her legs, and the phone in both hands. A space between the curtains let in a column of bright light behind her head and turned it into a dark cut-out shape.

"You say you prayers?"

"Since this morning." She pointed at the Bible on the nightstand.

"Get up and get ready fi school. I going wake Tony."

Anthony's door was open and Ronald looked in. His son was buried under two Transformers battling in bright blue space with white twinkling stars. Only a thin hand proved there was a boy there. Ronald stepped in the room, reached under the cosmos and held his son's foot, then let it go and stepped back to the door to watch him. He tried to remember when he had slept so, body askew, someone else taking care of things. Anthony turned in the bed, sending a ripple through space. Ronald felt like he was intruding, left the room, and continued to the bathroom.

∽

When she got to her family's pew, Shereen stopped for a moment, smiled, and gave a thumbs-up next to the bouquet of off-white lilies. Ronald gave two thumbs up, but Shereen had already gone as she walked along the center aisle to "Ode to Joy." The organza hem of her white dress skimmed the floor. Marva smiled and raised one eyebrow. Ronald read her face: *Shereen look the best.* When the bridal party reached the front of the church, the music stopped and Pastor Columbus took the mic.

"This is the day that the Lord has made. Let Jacqueline and Thomas rejoice and be glad in it." He raised both hands in the air and looked up at the ceiling. In his white suit with the silver embroidered waistcoat, Columbus looked like Elvis, and Ronald bent his head to hide his laughter. Since Columbus had transferred the title of the house to him and his wife, and they owned the deed, Ronald found the short, brocaded pastor and his probably-was-a-retired-ho wife comical. *How come mi never see it before?* was the question he kept asking himself. When he raised his head, Jacqueline and Thomas were kneeling before Columbus, who hovered one hand over both their heads and began to pray, "Almighty God. Today we have…"

Ronald stopped listening. Jacqueline looked small next to Thomas, a tall, handsome man who had only joined the church three months before. Everyone—not everyone, just Marva and Felix and Shereen—called

Thomas "the dark horse," he who had come out of nowhere and won Jacqueline. Ronald and Marva agreed that it was Columbus making the marriage happen. Shereen said it was Jacqueline's mother, but Ronald couldn't picture that slight, soft-spoken woman from Jamaica marrying her only daughter to a stranger.

"You may now kiss the bride," Columbus said into the mic. "Arrhhh, save some for later eh, Thomas. She is all yours."

Ronald craned his neck to see better. Thomas had bent Jacqueline backward and swallowed her lips with his. Jacqueline was either trying to push Thomas away with her thin, lace-encased arms or she was trying to put her palms against his chest. It was hard to tell. People laughed and some began to applaud. The claps caught like a fever until the entire church was clapping. Then, Thomas raised Jacqueline up, held her hand, and turned to face the audience.

"The mic still on?" Columbus said to someone at the front. "May I present to you. Mister. And. Missus. Thomas James Tourney."

Applause.

Pastor raised one hand and motioned for everyone to stand. "And before the lovely couple depart, I just want to acknowledge the bridal party." He pointed at the four bridesmaids. "Look how lovely they are. Like virginal brides. Brides in Christ."

Applause.

"And I think one of these lovely young women

will be here before me soon taking the wedding vows." Columbus paused. "Brother Davis, you know what I'm talking about."

The warmth in Ronald's chest rose to his face. From the pew in front, Sister Lewis and someone he didn't know turned around and smiled at him and Marva.

"But I don't want to let the pussy out of the bag, as they say." Columbus covered his mouth and widened his eyes as if he had said something he didn't mean to say. A few people laughed, sudden and loud. Their laughter bolted up to the ceiling like geysers.

"We let the couple depart. Play the procession." Columbus pointed one finger at the back of the church and music started.

Outside, newly budded trees had turned April a bright green. In places, small piles of gray snow waded in black water puddles. Ronald and his family went through the gate and stood on the sidewalk to watch Jacqueline's mother stuff the train of her daughter's dress into a shiny black car. People talked over the sound of sirens. Car horns played odd music along the avenue, car doors opened and closed. Ronald was still skimming this after-wedding world when an acrid smell burned his nostrils near the bridge and left a bitter taste in his mouth. He looked up. Dark gray pillow after dark gray pillow of smoke ate up the blue overhead. Sirens drowned out the after-wedding noises.

"You put the new one in a basin a water?" Marva whispered to him.

"Is not we." Ronald looked up Church Avenue.

"It look like it coming from 'round 39th." Marva's cheekbones jutted out at him. "You close the window? The curtain could ketch if it open. You close it?"

He searched his mind for the scene where he filled the basin with water, parted the curtain, pulled down the window, and moved the lever till he heard a click. "Mi don't know."

"You close it or not? O God, Ronnie. Talk."

"Mi don't know." He walked in the direction of the smoke.

When he turned onto 35th Street, the smell was even stronger, and smoke burned his nostrils and eyes. Hot wind blew into his face. Fire trucks blocked the street and he couldn't get close. He felt light-headed and sat on the pavement. He heard his heart beating in his ears and remembered something he had read about how breathing slowly helped situations like this, so he focused on Marva's calves, two shapely balusters that held up her coat, and counted each breath. By number twenty, he felt better. A little after that, he was somewhere else, and Marva's calves were the only two things in the world.

❧

A month after the fire, while they were still in church housing, they sent the children to relatives in Jamaica. With the children gone, they hardly spoke. Ronald felt his wife blamed him for the fire though she never said so. He felt other things too, but they were hard to put into words. One night, Marva interrupted their silent bed with a whisper that she felt watched in lodgings controlled by Cleopatra and her women's group, who visited once a week to tidy and drop off donations.

"Like di walls-dem listening," he whispered back.

They whispered more and laughed that night on a shared pillow until Ronald slid his hand across the isthmus of her waist.

She guided his hand to the space between them, then interlocked her fingers with his. "In we place. Promise."

He nodded as if he understood and, with one finger, traced the latitude where her head tie met her forehead until she smiled and her eyes glistened in the filtered streetlight coming through the thin discount store curtains. After she fell asleep, he tried to interpret her words. *She not comfortable ridin' in a borrow room in a house fi people in trouble? You not a man 'cause you can't provide a house fi we. Mi can't bring mi self to touch you till you do better. You can't touch mi till...* He didn't sleep that night.

Within a month, he found a rental on Eastern Parkway. They left their borrowed room as if going to work and didn't return. That evening, Marva video-called the children and gave a tour of the three-bedroom. There was laughter and shrieking as they tried to explain things to Marva's mother who kept asking, "Mek dem do it so?" about everything in the apartment.

After the call, Marva started crying. Ronald hugged her and found that he couldn't let her go. They ended up on the living room floor, their clothes as bedding. At first, they faced each other, then, without warning, Marva straddled him. He tried to sit up to embrace her but she pressed both hands on his chest and kept him down. She moved mechanically, and ground his sacrum into the varnished wooden floor, then jerked her head back, a tremor along the median of her stomach and chest. She got up without looking at him and went to the bathroom. Her sobs, then the sound of the shower. Since then, that was the only way they did it. He felt Marva said words with her body that she couldn't form with her mouth. He had only eight words for her, but never found the opportunity to say them: *Mi did tell you not to do it.*

⤚

Days later, they went to the New Community Church for the last time. They were initially headed toward the train station but passed it and walked all the way. It was warm and Brooklyn was alive with bright clothing, music from cars, and the heat of summer.

"Ronald? You daydreaming?" Marva touched him on the shoulder, as they waited outside.

"A lickle." He smiled and looked at the door beyond the wrought-iron gate. "Ready fi it?"

"You go. I go wait outside here till you come out."

Ronald shrugged and looked with envy at the blue

sky that had cleansed itself of gray smoke. White cotton wool clouds jeered at him.

Marva folded her arms and leaned against the gate. He pressed the buzzer.

The church office was a square, wood-paneled room with framed pictures of Columbus, Cleopatra, and the church elders. The young woman behind the desk got up as soon as Ronald walked in. "Mr. Davis." She shook his hand. "I is Annie Evers. Take a seat if you want." She pointed to a fat brown chair in front of the desk. "I go get the papers." She went into the file room next to the desk.

She returned and opened a manila folder on the table in front of him. "These is copies of the original policy with the church and these"—she took out five opened envelopes—"is all the correspondence from the insurance company about the investigation and about filing a claim about…am…the fire."

He raised an eyebrow and passed a finger along the cut in one of the envelopes.

"They sent them here because they didn't know how to get in touch with you while you was in the shelter. And the church address was listed as a next address. I open all the mail. Automatically. To sort it."

"Mi know. Is just—"

A woman screamed. Ronald felt like cold water was poured on his head and stood.

Annie froze then backed away.

The woman screamed again. "Marva." Ronald

looked around the office for a way out. "How mi get to di church?"

Annie covered her mouth with one hand and pointed at the file room.

Ronald went through the door at the other end of the file room then along a corridor to another door. Behind it, he heard Marva's screams and men's voices. He opened it and ran in.

At the front of the church, Columbus held Marva's hair with one hand and Felix and Winston held her arms. With his other hand, Columbus hit Marva with a fiber broom with a wooden handle, while reciting a prayer. About seven people, men and women, stood near Marva. The men's lips moved fast as they read aloud from open Bibles.

Ronald ran toward his wife and, at the same moment, Columbus roared, "Hold him."

Ronald was held at the shoulders and wrists. He could only see white gloves at his shoulders, and when he turned, there were faces covered in white gauze.

"Watch, Brother Davis, as I rebuke the spirit that has possessed your wife." Each time Columbus hit her with the small broom, she squealed. The broom had a red tassel with a bell that chimed each time Marva was struck. Ronald counted each chime, as he tried to pull free from the stewards. He swung his legs forward to gain momentum but couldn't get away.

After a few moments, Marva got quiet and only Columbus's voice echoed in the near-empty church.

"Tell me why you sought Satan through idols and candles?"

"I don't know." Marva's voice was like a child's.

"God has punished you. He take your house, eh. For taking the path of Saul, eh. For taking your family down the path of Saul. Say you accept Christ, the son of God, as your Lord and Savior."

She said it.

"Say it again."

She did.

"A third time so I know the evil spirit has left you."

"I accept Christ as my Lord and Savior. Christ is the son of God."

Columbus gave the broom to one of the Bible readers. Felix and Winston let her go and she dropped to her knees. Columbus and all his attendants backed away. The grip on Ronald's shoulders ended.

He went to Marva and helped her to stand. She held on to him as they walked toward the side door where he had come in. Columbus said something but Ronald didn't listen.

"Marv—"

"How?" Marva asked when they were in the corridor.

"Insurance papers." Ronald wiped the wetness from her face.

"You have them?"

"In di office."

"We get them and go." Her voice had regained its strength.

In the office, Annie leaned against one wall with her arms folded across her chest. Ronald closed the folder on the desk and took it.

"Dis all? All di papers you have fi we."

"Yes," the secretary said.

Ronald walked toward her and raised one arm as if he was going to hit her.

"Yes, is all. Everything." She ducked and ran to the other side of the room.

Ronald and Marva closed the wrought-iron gate behind them and held each other as they walked toward the Nostrand Avenue train station, headed for home and another life.

"All sin born outta love enno. All."

— HECTOR, JUST BEFORE HE WAS DIAG-
NOSED WITH THROAT CANCER AND
LOST THE ABILITY TO EAT, SING, TELL
ANYONE ELSE WHAT HAPPENED, 1991

Drink the Dew

THE FIRST TIME I see she, I was leading a gang of workers to pave the street in front of she grandmother house in Scarborough.

She did live there with she mother, Miss Betty. The house was brick on six short, concrete piles and had fancy wooden decorations, like them houses in colonial times, and a gallery at the side. It was inland but the salty sea blas' from the harbor eat away the galvanize roof and leave blackish teeth marks on the roof curly edge. Most of the time, the two women keep the wooden jalousies close so the workers can't see inside the house. But sometimes, she, the daughter, would open one jalousie a lil' bit and look out for hours. From the road, she look like a cotton shape with wooden stripes and no face. Then just so, the jalousie would be shut for days and, from church bell to whistle blow, me and the workmen search the wooden eyelids a the house for a glimpse a she.

Then, one morning she appear in the gallery with a jug and call we for water. She was shapely, tall and strong, with a mannishness to she. A plain face that I didn't know how to read yet. She pour my water without looking at me, turn and gone inside. That was how Queenie was. All she actions flow into one another, like river into sea. She was the mouth a the river. You could never know how deep she was. This was the real reason I did love she, though I never use that word.

After the road finish, I visit she a few times. Miss Betty was there plenty times, sitting at one corner of the gallery, crocheting some endless doily and sucking she teeth. Queenie sit down across from me, a glass of lime juice on the table between we, nodding she head, not saying nothing. Me, talking more than I ever talk. 'Bout people in Hope Village, where I born and grow. Who marry. Who buying land. Then I start to talk 'bout myself, boasting about my land in the village interior, 'bout my salary and all the people who work under me, feeling like I have to impress Queenie and she mother. This go on for three weeks or so until one morning I was going there on my bicycle with a peccary I did ketch that dawn and, jus' so, I turn around and ride to John Dial, the village just before Hope, to a one-room house on four concrete piles. There was a separate kitchen, flat on the ground at the left of the house.

In John Dial, Katie was in the backyard hanging out clothes. I could see she legs, thick and solid. I call out to she from the street, but she didn't answer. She stand up still, listening, not knowing I could see she. Overhead, a kiskadee scream as it fly out from the dry gully at the back of Katie house. She come out to meet me and clap she hands.

Hector, yuh bring a peccary fi mi, or yuh on yuh way to someplace else? A wire bend across she forehead, but a bell was ringing in she voice.

I dey here. I smile.

She clap again and take the animal from me, the wire gone from between she eyes.

I don't say nothing more to Katie. She leave the clothes and make a fire near the kitchen. As I was bathing in the open air on the concrete slab near the gully, I smell the smokey, sweaty stinkness of she singeing the hair from the peccary. I put on the same clothes and hang out the rest of she washing. When she done cook, we eat, me sitting on a crate and she standing at the kitchen door. Afterwards, just so, without even washing she hands and mouth, she lift she skirt to show she front to me. I didn't really want any, but I was generous with the peccary, so she feel she had to be generous with she self. I take a little with my head turn to one side so she can't kiss me.

❧

After that, I stay off Cane Street and any of the streets near where Queenie live with she mother. It was easy too, 'cause the government was cutting more roads in town, and I get another foreman post. It was 1946, you see. The war was over by then, and the big boys from England and Trinidad did want to develop Tobago after they did neglect we for so long. Some people say it was the distance and the cost of the steamer to travel between the two islands. But I think it was that Port-of-Spain was far away, and Tobago was just a village to them big boys making decisions from nice offices in the capital with fans and ice water.

Was so then. Same now.

I think, altogether, I didn't see Queenie for nearly two months. So, when Ottley youngest boy come all the way from town to bring the message that she want to see me, I was in two minds about going. I give the boy ten cents for the message and get on my bicycle.

Nobody was in the yard, so I lean my cycle against the side of the house. I look up at the jalousie and was starting to feel that feeling again. You know? Like a boy playing among he betters. But I straighten up my back and walk up them three concrete steps. Nobody in the gallery, and the drawing-room door was open, so I walk in. In the drawing room, I just make out the shapes of cabinets and chairs in the false dawn inside. Uneasy, I hold on to the hem of my shirt at the back then I hear something behind me. When I turn, Queenie was there in a thin cotton duster. The light from the open front door make the duster into whitish glass, and I could see she full, bare breasts underneath. I slap she hard on she waist with one hand like I was sizing up a tree before

I cut it down. She turn, close the door, and we do we quick, scorching thing right there.

⤦

When we get together, I move out from Tan house to live with Queenie and she mother. After each of the first three boys, Sidney, James, and Phillip, was born, Betty take care of Queenie. Band-up Queenie belly and gave she bush to drink, so the body would come back to itself after the babies.

Just around after Phillip was born, Betty marry a Horace James, a man from right down the road from where we live. With money from the goods Horace sell from he garden, together with what Betty save from she job in Scarborough General, washing dirty bedding and clothes, they build a house together on Horace family land. Fast, fast they had a son. Then a boy and girl twin. Betty did ease off visiting we for lil' bit, as she settle sheself and she new marriage. After we daughter, Freda, was born, Betty start to visit more often, staying longer each time. Sometimes she bring she three chirren and spend weeks away from she own house and husband. I think things wasn't going good between she and Horace, 'cause sometimes I see him in town and, since the twin, he get small.

With all the chirren, mine, plus Betty three sometimes, I hire a woman, Carol, to help with the cooking and washing. Most evenings, I come home to quarrels that finish just as I was parking my cycle behind the house. By the time I reach inside, Betty leave the room quick, mumbling to she self as she go. Queenie, like always, didn't let Betty tune strum she.

❧

We was together five years and Betty was still bad-mouthing.

She say I have other women.

How I didn't have enough money.

How I was too ugly for she daughter.

Sometimes, I did feel to spin Betty around and put some bad words in she face. Let she know how I was the best man for she daughter. But Betty was a starch-cotton-and-hat kind of woman, and it was easy to imagine these things when she was not in the same room. In she face, I couldn't find my voice. This was about the time Queenie ask me to build a house for we alone.

We will rent out this house I inherit from my grandmother, so it stay in the family. That way people go stay in their own house.

It was the first time she almost say something about Betty being with we all the time.

I had land all over Hope and choose a nice plot almost to the center of the village. Betty would have had to leave the pave street and follow a dirt path along Hope River to get to it. Ha!

Queenie was pregnant with Henry, we last chile, when I start as foreman on a government project to cut and pave new roads in Roxborough. I and men from the village was putting in work at the new house most eve-nings during the week and on weekends. When I did go to Queenie, it was to sleep or to wash and cook when Carol was off. Queenie got fat, round, and nice. Things was good between we. We had we own way of talking without words when Betty was there. Sometimes, we talk with we eyes and leave Betty with the chirren so we could make fierce love in the small kitchen next to the house. All my sons was toy versions of me, tall, broad-shoulders with laugh lines that go from both sides of their noses to the corner of their mouths. Freda, with she Demerara sugar hair color and fair skin, look jus' like Queenie, move like she, but had a big ocean-like way about she. She wasn't a river mouth at all. Freda was someone you could know.

❧

That morning, I did wake up early, early to play with the chirren before I leave for work. When I walk up from the bathroom behind the house, a stiff brackish wind was blowing off the harbor, so I hug my damp skin and wait for Queenie to open the door. She did just finish nursing Henry and hand him to me. We hear a grumble, as we pass through the drawing room where Betty and she three chirren sleep on the floor, and stifle a giggle. I get dress and talk soft to Queenie about the house in the interior. Henry, at nine months, was trying to walk, and the boys get up from their bedding under we bed to hug my neck and play. Freda sit at the edge of the bed staring. I ask she what she was looking at and she cover she face. She keep it cover up till I leave for work.

In town, the shipment of pitch to pave the road was keep back in Trinidad, so I send the men home and ride to Friendsfield Road, sit down on a metal railing by the side of the road to smoke a Du Maurier. Errol, a fella from Hope, who I see around town, stop and ask me for cigarettes. Errol talk through two cigarettes, then get quiet. I don't remember what I ask him or how we get to it, but he tell me if I go home now, I go see Queenie with she man. After he say it, he jump off the railing like if somebody push him and hold up he two hands, like he was surrendering.

I throw the rest of the cigarettes at him and get on my bicycle. I wasn't feeling the handlebars or the pedals. My body was moving from memory.

When I reach there, Betty was under the house with Freda and the twin. She run toward me and shout out Queenie name. I push Betty, take my cutlass from the house post and run up the steps. My heart was boiling in my chest. I was sweating, the air like just before a storm. My body tingling like I was hunting and about to corner a 'gouti.

In the gallery, Queenie was by the front door and, for the first time, I could read she.

Behind she was a man. I try to get pass she, but she block the doorway. Then, I don't know, I feel to bathe she, so I try to take she to the bathroom and, when she wouldn't go, I hit she with the side of the cutlass, hold she hand and drag she on she belly down the stairs and around to the bathroom at the back of the house. The man, I can't say he name, jump over the low banister and run away. In the bathroom, I throw a bucket of water on she and ask, Wha' you doin'?

I don't know. Is, is Mammy. She was crying and the spit and phlegm make a bubble when she say it.

She face and chest was scrape-up—dress tear-up. Heavy footsteps pound my head and chest. Me and she was the only people in the world. I close my eyes and when I open them, Queenie, the bathroom, the yard, the house, everything was behind a door, and I was looking at them through a small hole, seeing only glimpses of things, never the whole picture. Next, it was like I did just wake up—hands, feet, head, every part of me tired and heavy. My throat hurt, and I was trying to remember something that was at the tip of my tongue. The side of my face was itching and when I scratch it, my fingers was bloody. It was all over my chest, my pants, my boots. I was in the front yard looking for Queenie 'cause I did just come home from somewhere and wanted to tell she something. Then, my boot hit she head, done cover up with bluebottle flies. She was split down she center, she insides mix up with grass and dirt. Between she legs, a bloody pulp. I roar hard to bring down the sky so it would flatten me 'cause I spoil she. When the sky didn't fall, I put the cutlass to my throat and rub it back and forth, a damp, rubbery noise in my ears. Sounds from far away get closer. Hands hold me down, grab the blade and hit me till I was out.

❧

I spend most of the court case trying to remember what happen between the railing and finding Queenie so. I listen to the lawyer man with the white wig, the constable, Betty in black. All of them talking and talking. But they was talking about scenes from a magic lantern show that I never see when the man from Trinidad come to set up he complicated business in the market in town. In the end, I get manslaughter—five years on Carrera Island. People say I didn't hang 'cause Betty was the only witness. Betty encourage wrongdoing, they say. Bible justice.

Upholding, Horace tell she, just as they was carrying me out, chain up like a animal.

They say too that I get five years 'cause my mother dress a fowl cock with obeah to sway the judge. Tan would do something like that, but I could never ask, 'cause obeah have no conversation.

The chirren scatter, some to this one, others to that one.

When they release me and I was back in Hope, my daddy give me the house he used to live in with the woman he marry after he and Tan mash up. I was there a week when Betty drop Sidney, James and Phillip in the street and leave before I could walk to the place where the Barber-Green meet the dirt in my yard. I couldn't look at them boys without my eyes burning and thinking about the darkness after the cigarette on the bridge that make them not have a mother. Not too long after, Leonard, Queenie daddy, bring Freda and Henry on the front of he bicycle with their bedding and school books in a flour bag tie to the back. At eight years old, Freda was the mirror of she mother in face and almost in body. But that wasn't the reason I send she to live with Tan. The house was one room then. Me and four boys? Not proper for she. Freda had a long, bumpy scar on she stomach that she scratch sometimes. When I ask she 'bout it, she say it was always there. I know she get that mark somewhere in the twilight between jumping off a bicycle in the middle of the day and trying to cut my own throat.

Once me and the chirren was back in Hope, things settle into a rhythm. Steady. Like waves back and forth on Hope Beach. Freda with Tan. Me carrying food there every week to help out. Bonito, Moonshine, 'guana, cassava, anything I ketch or plant. Freda does come to play with she brothers after school or on a Saturday evening after she wash she school clothes and anything else Tan ask she to do. The boys spend time between me and Betty and their endless fighting. Sydney and Phillip was alright, but James. Greedy and often picking at people. At things. At ants, for walking near he foot. From he small, he had a thing in him I didn't like. Henry stay, say 'bout three months, then gone back to Leonard and Ann, he common-law wife, in Scarborough. I try to tell him, I is he daddy and these is he brothers, but I read he eyes from the first day he reach and them eyes was always asking: Who is these people?

I did stop dreaming after it happen, then just so I was having the same dream every night. I looking for somebody or something or someplace I can't find. I wake from this searching dream with a deep, deep disappointment that make me vex they take away my cutlass so quick. Then I was shame that God know what I thinking. Since they release me from Carrera, my throat is dry all the time, a thirstiness I can't get rid of. So, I drink. Rum. Drink till the dryness gone, till I fall, grateful for sleep without the endless searching and finding nothing.

I sell the half-finish house and gamble away some of the land. I beat the boys sometimes 'cause I can't beat myself.

As to women. Well. Nobody for a long time. But I have property and draw pay, and that is enough for them with chirren to mind and who want to eat their yam with salted cod instead of salted butter sometimes. When the feeling is more than me and there is no one, I go to Katie. She only let me in she house at night, but I have to leave before bird wife wake up. Eventually, I take up with one Charlene. She live in a three-room with she mother and three brothers. Men go in and out to the mother when things was tight with them. Charlene was meager and short for a woman with open sores on she hands and feet, hardly talk and didn't ask questions. At first, like everybody else, I climb in she bedroom window at night for one thing. Then for other things. I start washing she sores with Bluestone to dry up the weeping and to take away the smell she had. Feed she Marmite and Horlicks with boil cow milk. One night I notice she body was fuller, warmer. That same night after we finish, she mother come in the room, sit down on the only chair, and look down at we, lying on the floor on rice bags stuff with grass.

Belly ah tell pussy secret, Mr. Scott, she say. Yuh ah go claim mi only daugh'tah?

I look from Charlene to she mother and nod yes. Another direction.

I add on a room to the house and take Charlene there. We start a family, grafting a thin failing branch to a strong tree with termites eating the root. Freda and she brothers, I keep close in the breast pocket of my shirt, as me and Queenie was together in them. Proof that there was another direction at one time.

Sometimes I see Betty in town. In the market usually. She tall loud daughter and quiet knotty sons and husband in tow. She still don't talk to me. And she does make a point to turn she back when she see me. Sometimes, I watch she back muscles tense up under the cotton as she turn away. Sometimes, I turn away too, my hands shaking and needles sticking me all over.

Bruk Pocket
Special
$2.99
Chicken meals only

— Entry in Paula's journal,
26 September, 1995

Exile

THE DAY PAULA arrived in Brooklyn, a Sunday in late August, the rain came down in gray arrows that covered the windows of the livery cab she rode in like a cloth. She could only make out the shapes of buildings, like dark teeth in a fog. It rained for the entire week, and she didn't leave her room at the top of the stairs in the brownstone where she stayed with her aunt Lorna. On Friday, when the rain stopped, she looked through the window at the world to which she was exiled until her belly, which still looked like she'd had too much to eat, had disappeared. The world across the street was a white brownstone with brown trim and an empty lot with a long blue car with tufts of grass where the wheels should be.

She was interrupted by the slide then click of Lorna's key in the front door, her puttering in the living room, and her feet ascending the stairs.

Lorna knocked.

"Open." Paula turned to face the door.

Her aunt walked in—the broad beam of her hips swaying with each stride—and sat on the bed next to her.

"I not going to ask you if you alright today, 'cause I know you not alright," she began. "You fifteen years old. Pregnant. And Phyllis and Andy send you away to hide you."

"Is not…" Tears slid across her upper lip and into her mouth. "Is not that…" It was that her aunt had said her mother's name and she remembered when the doctor told her the news. Her mother cried and held her chest like someone had cuffed her in it. Since that day, her mother had stopped speaking to her and she only heard her mother's voice, high-pitched and clear, when her parents talked in their bedroom at night.

"Look. I know my sister," Lorna continued. "School principal. Big in the church. Treasurer of the Lions Club. You the spitting image of her when she was your age. Bright in school. Nice hair. Good looking. In my sister mind, this not happening." She moved a hair from Paula's forehead. "She still talk like the nuns in the convent? I will not!" She paused. "Tolerate that!" Lorna put her hands on her hips and lifted her chest to feign perfect posture.

"We will *not!* speak about it again," Paula said, pursing her lips for effect, straightened her back and lifted her chest.

Just so, they laughed. Paula's chuckle that ended

in a hiss and her aunt's loud cackle sounded strange together. Lorna slapped her thigh and got silent, her face still and serious. "Now, your mother is a little"— she winked and touched the tips of two fingers together like she was holding something tiny—"much. But she want the best for you. She want you to have a future. My sister can't handle it. She couldn't even bring herself to ask me to see about you. Only Andy been calling. And they plan to take care of you, darling. Clothes. Hospital bill. Everything. You understand?"

"Yes."

"You going to have a life when you go back to Trinidad. Your father been calling late at night to tell me all that going on. You do your part. And just know that I will see about everything here. You hear me?"

"Yes." Paula wondered what her part was.

"Good girl. Now come, let we make dinner, nah? Me and you." She had a crease above one eye. "You can't just stay in this room all the time watching out the window."

"Okay." Paula took one last look at the car across the street and stood.

～

Her aunt accompanied her to the first two visits to the prenatal clinic. On the way back from the third visit, Paula was to take the 2 train to Church and Nostrand, then take a taxi from the line of cars along Nostrand to the house. When she got to Nostrand, the drivers were arguing because one of them skipped the line and took a passenger before his turn. She decided to walk. It was a warm day in late September and many people walked along Church Avenue. The avenue was the sound of horns and bus engines, reggae and soca blasting from cars and a speaker box on the corner at Nostrand near the McDonald's. It was the smell of jerk pit smoke, incense, trays of apples, cantaloupes, and onions that jutted toward her hip. Store signs so close together that they read like a run-on sentence: *Beauty Supply Money Transfer/Bill Pay Barbados $297, RT, Tops 3 for $10*. It started raining when she turned onto 36th—big drops that hit her head like pebbles. A smell, like moist earth and gasoline, caused her mouth to fill with saliva. At the top of the unpainted concrete steps, she fumbled with the keys. A bubbly feeling shot up from her stomach, and she leaned over the painted metal railing and vomited on the cover of a black garbage bin at the side of the steps. The rain broke up the pinkish vomit like lights going out in a city at night. She opened the door, held her chest, and leaned against the red-flowered wallpaper in the vestibule until the nausea and dizziness passed. On the floor, among the restaurant menus and letters that were slipped through the mail slot, she found a letter from her mother. In it were photocopies of prayers, novenas to the Virgin Mary for the safety of mothers and children. She checked the envelope twice. Nothing more. After her bath, she wrote a response to the letter she wished her mother had sent. She read what she had written, tore it up, and decided to start a journal. In the back of a new notebook, she put a flier about safe drinking water she had picked up at the clinic that morning and a menu from a restaurant she passed on the way. On the first page, she wrote the words from a sign in front of a restaurant that advertised daily specials. After, she started a novel from among the books her father had packed for her to study with for her exams when she returned, *A House for Mr. Biswas*.

∽

About an hour later than the usual time, Lorna's key turned in the door. There was a man with her. Paula put the novel on her chest and waited. She wanted to hide, and her eyes darted around the room to find a place. She stood and went to the mirror to see if her belly showed through her cotton shirt. She let Lorna call twice before she answered.

"Yes, Auntie."

"Come down a minute." There was a laugh in her voice.

Paula took the steps one at a time. She didn't want to appear eager.

Lorna and the man were standing together at the base of the steps. He was two heads taller than her aunt and had an arm across her upper back. His fingers played with her shoulder.

"Paula, this is Rawle. My boyfriend." Lorna glanced at him.

"Nah true, I'm her man." Rawle held out his hand

to Paula. He had a broad face and the skin around his mouth was soft and loose. "Nice to meet you, young lady." He smiled and four lines bracketed his mouth.

Lorna explained that she and Rawle taught at the same school. Rawle taught math.

"We don't just teach together." Rawle gave her a flier. "Lorna don't tell you? We sing together." He winked and lines filled one side of his face. "We sing backup for soca and reggae artistes."

The flier was black with the faces of Mighty Sparrow, David Rudder, and Black Stalin surrounded by pink and blue fireworks with the words *Soca Celebration* at the top.

"You coming to that," Lorna said and touched Paula's cheek.

Lorna cooked rice and peas with stewed chicken for dinner, and they ate together on the black leather couches in the living room. Paula went up to her room while her aunt and Rawle talked in the kitchen. There, she put the soca flier in her journal then lay listening to her aunt and her boyfriend in the kitchen. She couldn't make out any of the words, just the bass of Rawle's voice and their laughter. She thought that her parents rarely sounded like the two people in the kitchen. Her mother once told her that Lorna didn't live a Catholic life. Paula wondered if she was sent to live with Lorna because she belonged there. Keep the sinners together. Downstairs got quiet and she strained her ear to listen but couldn't hear anything. She fell asleep reading the part where Mohun passes the note to the girl in the shop.

༂

6 October 1995

*Here, I am more myself. The self I am in school with
my friends. The self that Isaac knows. Auntie asks
me what I think and discusses things with me. She
involves me in her life with Uncle Rawle and the
singing and stuff. This is kind of surprising because
we don't even play soca in the house at home. I'm sure
none of the family in Trinidad knows that Auntie sings
soca and reggae. I went to one of Auntie's rehearsals.
It was filled with older people from different islands,
who I would probably never have met if I wasn't in
Brooklyn. They were nice. Most of them were trying
not to look at my big belly. I felt funny and just stayed
near the wall at the front of the room.*

*I compare Mummy and Daddy to Uncle Rawle and
Auntie. Uncle Rawle is Jamaican. Mummy used
to say that people from the other islands, especially
Jamaicans, are no good. At home, Mummy talks.
Daddy and I listen and do. That's how I ended up
here. I should have said something. Asked questions
or made some kind of a fuss when I realized that they
were sending me away. I am like Mohun Biswas.
Things happened TO him. He didn't make decisions
to guide his own life. He gave a girl a note and was
married to her. Then the Tulsis took over his life. I
don't want my life to be like that.*

New Idea #1: I will not let people, including my parents, make me do things I don't want to do without a discussion and without knowing all the facts. (This does not include things pertaining to my education and things like getting a job and so forth.)

I have been in the States since 27 August, and no one, not Mummy, not Daddy, not Isaac, has called me to ask me how I'm doing. Auntie gives updates to my parents about me, and she gives me updates about them. Who is giving Isaac updates?

New Idea #2: I will not be waiting for things to happen to me. I WILL BE HAPPENING TO THINGS. I will buy a phone card and call my parents. I will also call Isaac to let him know what's going on with me.

New Idea #3: Ask Daddy what will happen when I get back to Trinidad.

News: My due date is 14 January 1996.

Exercises

Leg lifts: 4 sets of 10

Arms: 3 sets of 10 for biceps and shoulders (each) with tin of condensed milk (10 oz)

Step ups: 3 sets of 10

CXC Exams

- *Looked over literature syllabus*
- *Did past paper questions about* Biswas
- *Started* Things Fall Apart
- *Did a whole mathematics past paper. Uncle Rawle corrected it. I got a 95, which means I'll get a 1 in maths. Of course!*
- *History: Read Chapters 1 and 2*

Paula re-read her writing then placed a red sycamore leaf between the pages of the journal and closed it.

∽

From the kitchen, the phone echoed through the two-story house like the high-pitched bleat of a mechanical sheep. Her aunt had just left for work and Paula was in the living room nursing a cup of orange peel tea to suppress her nausea. The answering machine came on. After the greeting, a man's voice said, "Hello. Paula. Is Daddy. Well, I'm—"

She picked up the phone. "Daddy?"

"Paula?"

"Is me. Something happen?" She was planning to call her parents that day.

"No. I just wanted to see how you going." He took a deep, noisy breath.

"I going good. Fine. How you? How Mummy?" She was happy to hear his voice.

"I alright. Cool, not fussy." He paused. "Your mum. Well. She good. Coping."

"What she coping with?" Her voice was louder than she meant. Then she realized that she meant her voice to be loud, so she repeated the question.

"With everything. She just trying to cope, Paula." More loud breathing into the phone.

"She coping with me, ent?"

"Paula, you think I want to send my only child away? But it is the best solution. The best way for you to have a life when this is all over. Me and your mother want the best for you. You understand?"

On the drive to the airport, her father had kept the radio on from Plaisance Park to Piarco, and hardly spoke to her. While she weighed her luggage and checked in, he circled at a distance, like a corbeau waiting for something to die. Just before she went through the departure gate, he ran to the head of the line and hugged her. "Don't worry." He smelled like Brut and ironed cotton. "You will come back, and everything will work out." He held her against his chest and patted her head. His wedding ring was against her ear, an island of hardness surrounded by warm flesh.

She didn't understand. "Daddy. I want to know something. Tell me the truth, alright?"

"Alright." He sighed and she pictured the air from his nostrils ruffling the hairs of his moustache.

"When you say I will have a life when this is all

over, you mean I will live my life as if I didn't have a child?"

"Once a person has a child, they could never live like they never had one. Most people never recover from having a child at a young age. They never finish school. Don't get decent work. But we, me and your mother, want you to recover. We don't want a situation where a person ends up spending the rest of their life paying for something that happen when they were young."

"But is me, Daddy. Me, Paula, who going to have a baby."

"I know."

"But you not saying it. You keep saying is a person." Her temples hurt.

Another sigh. "I get what you saying."

She waited to hear if he'd say more, but there was silence as if the phone had gone dead.

"You there?" she asked.

"I right here."

"Daddy, you and Mummy plan to send the baby to an orphanage when I get home and pretend that I never had one?" The pain in her temples was now at her neck and she touched her stomach, hoping the feeling would not get to the baby.

"Truth is, I don't know what we going to do when you come back. I only know that the nuns will hold a space for you to sit CXCs next year, and we will take it from there."

He sounded tired, worn. She said okay, and changed

the subject to the weather and the different Caribbean accents in Brooklyn. She ended their conversation when the fatigue had left his voice and he sounded sure about the future, like he did at the airport weeks ago.

After her father hung up, she called Isaac. He answered. He was a year ahead of her and was at home, taking a break after exams. He planned to start a job in Petrotrin after the New Year.

"So you really in the States, then?"

It was this way of seeming innocent, believing all that was said, and taking everything at face value that had drawn her to him. She laughed and, for a moment, they were at the Carnegie Free Library in San Fernando, kissing behind the big art book they called the kissing book, *Uffizi Collezioni*.

"I thought it was just talk. 'Cause I call your house a few times, looking for you. But whenever I ask to talk to you, please, your mom say you not there and hang up on me."

No one had mentioned Isaac calling for her. She was hurt. "When you call for me?"

"Like around the end of June."

By mid-June, still in Trinidad, she had started vomiting in the mornings, and had been able to hide it for over a week by throwing up in a plastic bag, crouched near the floor in her bedroom. Until one morning, on the drive to school, she retched her breakfast in the back seat and her mother turned around to face her. The vomit was caught in the hammock that her plaid uniform skirt made as it hung between her legs. The car stopped and Paula kept her eyes on the blue-and-green plaid marbled with puke as the stench—rancid food tinged with a sourness—filled the Toyota. "Paula?" was all her mother asked.

When Paula looked up, her mother's eyes were blinking fast, as if to clear the vision from her sight. It was panic and knowing. The next day, the doctor confirmed that she was ten weeks pregnant. By that evening, she was cut off from the world as her parents made arrangements. No school. No phone calls. No visitors. No leaving the house.

"That was nearly four months ago, Isaac." He didn't call every single day since her mother said she wasn't there, nor did he try to see her. She brushed the thought away. "What everybody saying I doing here?"

"That you in school. You got a scholarship to go to university because you got a really high score on the SATs. What school you going to?"

"I not in school, Izz. Remember that note I pass to you that day in ad maths lessons?" It was just two days before she vomited in the car. That day, he jumped in his father's Laurel as soon as lessons was over, so there was no time to talk.

"That was real?" His thin head got long and mis-shapen when his jaw dropped, and she knew that it was thoroughly deformed now.

"I pregnant. That is why I in the States."

A long silence. Then he spoke: "But I was planning to work in Petrotrin for a year or two, then start my own petroleum consulting business with my father. I didn't know the note was real. It say that what happen by Nalini house was making you vomit on mornings. Wasn't sure what…I was just…just calling your house 'cause we was supposed to go to graduation ball together, nah. And I didn't hear from you, so I end up going with Sally Sitahal, and now she and I kinda together and Dad looking for something in Petrotrin for she too, and I really…"

She let Isaac go on until the voice on the phone card said she had one minute remaining. She asked if he wanted her number. He took the number and asked for her mailing address. But the phone cut off before she could give him the zip code. She waited for him to call back, but he didn't.

∽

27 October 1995

I really, really, really LOVE Isaac. Like LOVE. I can't even put it into words. He's so nerdy and cute and funny. He looks just like Fido Dido, if Fido was real. I am crying. Sad.

I have hiccups.

Lorraine used to tell me that Sally was always looking at Isaac and that she liked him too. Graduation ball was in July. I wasn't allowed to go anywhere or use the phone. And he went with Sally sooooo quick. ~~It's as if he never to~~

~~They could even be doing it. I hate Sally. I will look~~
~~desperate if I called Sally.~~

∽

11 November 1995

*It's cold like in the fridge. I'm writing with the space
heater on, and I'm under the covers and still. Fall
was windy and rainy. Now there's no rain, and the
sun is so bright. If it wasn't for the branches of leafless
trees that look like sea fan coral against the grayish
blue sky, you would think it was summer and go
outside without a jacket.*

*I am seven months, and my belly feels heavy. Since
the first visit, the nurses in the clinic have been
asking if I wanted to know if I was having a boy or
a girl. I didn't want to know, but I have changed
my mind. When I go back next time, I will find
out.*

*My breasts are bigger. Lorraine and Sasha used to
say that if you let boys feel up your breasts, they will
get bigger. Issac ~~feeled~~ felt me up a lot before we did
the <u>thing itself</u> and my breasts never grew. Or L & S
were right, because feeling up leads to the <u>thing itself</u>
that gets you pregnant and THAT makes your breasts
bigger.*

Auntie and I went shopping for bras in Kings Plaza Mall. The mall is like Gulf City Mall, but with more stores.

I called Isaac again today. I was talking and he kept answering with one-word answers, so I got off the phone. He sounds stupid and probably looks dumb.

Auntie gave me coconut oil to rub on my belly, breasts, and hips so I wouldn't get any stretch marks. I started, but I stopped. The stretch marks will be like if I wrote this whole experience on my body. No one can erase it. It will be a metaphor (comparison without the use of like or as) for a journal.

New Idea #11: Do not do anything that will hide the fact that you had a child. Make sure to keep all the paperwork from the clinic and everything you get for the child.

In between my studies, I'm reading a book Uncle Rawle gave me, So You're Pregnant. *The book says that your emotions are higher when you're pregnant, and I think I am experiencing that. I am almost finished with* Things Fall Apart, *by* ~~Chinea~~ *Chinua Achebe, and everything in the book reminds me of things happening in real life, so I cry, then I'm angry and frightened. In personality, Okonkwo is definitely Mummy. Daddy could be any one of Okonkwo's wives, except Ekwefi. Ikemefuna is not exactly,*

exactly like me, but he comes the closest. He was sent away as a peace settlement to pay a debt. He was in exile like me. He got comfortable and started to think that New York was his home and that Auntie Lorna was his mother and Uncle Rawle was his father. Okonkwo played a part in killing the boy because he wanted to not be like his father. He didn't do the right thing. He did the perfect thing so that people would think he was perfect in every way. Mummy is always perfect. Okonkwo hurt his own feelings by killing the boy. I'm sure Mummy hurts her own feelings all the time. But I will never know.

New Idea #12: Forget what other people think about me. If I focus on what people think or on being perfect all the time, I will hurt my own feelings.

New Idea #13: Try to call Daddy more.

Jokes: (A child sitting next to me in the clinic told me.)

What do you call an ant who does magic tricks?

Tah-daaant!

Exercises

Leg lifts: 3 sets of 10

Arms: 3 sets of 12 for biceps and shoulders (each) with 8 lb. weights that we bought in Burlington

Coat Factory.

Step ups: 3 sets of 12 (with 8 lb. weights)

CXC

- *Need to do some more past paper questions in lit.*

- *Did 2 maths past papers. I got only 80. I don't understand matrices at all. If lots of matrices come, I might not do so good. Uncle Rawle has started tutoring me, but he and Auntie have already started rehearsals for the Christmas soca and calypso events that happen in Caribbean neighborhoods here. Soon, he wouldn't have much time to do it, so I'm taking lots of notes and going through the textbook on my own.*

- *Did 2 history past papers. Auntie will mark them this weekend.*

- *On the side, I started* Hamlet *but I don't always understand everything without Auntie explaining it. She is good at everything.*

❧

After the holiday concert in New Jersey, Paula went backstage. Lorna introduced her to some of the other backup singers, and some of the calypsonians. In Trinidad, she thought little of the men and women who sang calypso and soca. But in the States, these men and women, the lyrics and the music *were* Trinidad, *were* home. In the back seat of Rawle's car, her hand pulsed where David Rudder and the Mighty Shadow held it while they wiped their foreheads in the hot, crowded room backstage. She touched her belly with the hand so her child could feel Trinidad too.

The next morning, Paula walked into the kitchen and saw Rawle and Lorna kissing. She yelled, "Sorry," covered her mouth, and turned to go back upstairs.

Lorna called her back. "Come, Paula. Rawle just a little romantic this morning."

"Is the music," Rawle said and smiled. "It make me do it." He smoothed Lorna's hair.

"Miss Paula," Rawle began. "I want invite you to spend Christmas by my house. I'm a very good cook, and I hope you will come to eat and drink and meet my people."

"Yes, I'll come. But you don't have to ask me so formal." She was angry but wasn't sure why.

"We just thought is your choice," Rawle said.

"Is fine. I don't have anything else to do anyway." She lifted both shoulders then dropped them.

Lorna raised one bushy eyebrow. "You want some toast? Tea? We have Milo."

"I feel a lil' upset. Maybe some orange peel first. To settle my stomach." Her anger faded and she wanted to apologize. "I sorry, Uncle Rawle. Don't know why I acting so."

"You and me always cool," Rawle said.

"Is okay. Sit down in the drawing room. I go bring the tea." Lorna took a cup from the dish rack.

On the couch, Paula cried with her face in her hands. She missed Isaac and the future they had planned behind the kissing book. She hadn't called her father as much as she had promised in her journal, and found that she couldn't picture his face. After a few moments, there was a warm hand at the back of her neck, then her aunt held her. She kept her face in her hands and wished she could stay in that warmth forever.

❦

30 January 1996

Ikemefuna Andrew Rawlins Guevara was born on 12 January 1996 at 11:05 a.m.

Ikemefuna: So the boy Okonkwo raised could have a second chance at life, after the decision of the Oracle. And because my son was born in exile.

Andrew: After Daddy.

Rawlins: After Uncle Rawle because he is so nice to me. If and when I have a girl child, I will name her Lorna.

You can register the birth in Trinidad from here, as the baby has the same citizenship as the mother. I didn't put any name for father.

I. has not called me.

He looks like me and like I. He has my mouth and

complexion, and I.'s eyes with long lashes. I couldn't write for two weeks because everything was hurting so much. The birth itself was fine. I got an epidural like Auntie suggested, so the birth was something heavy pressing down on my hips, but from the inside. I had nice nurses and the doctor, Dr. Kenneth Brathwaite, was from Trinidad. I got five stitches and Dr. Brathwaite came personally to make sure I knew how to take care of them and that I understood everything. I think he felt sorry for me because he kept saying that I couldn't even "full up the bed." That it was too big for me. It was like having Daddy there.

Pain started after I got home and got worse when I nursed Ike. It was like big hands with sharp, pointy fingernails were scraping downward from my chest to my belly. Auntie said it was afterpains. She said that we are country people from Paramin Village. We have land and my grandparents and aunts and uncles minded pigs and bathed in the river. Apparently, I have many cousins and great aunts and uncles that my mother doesn't talk to. That we are mixed with Amerindian, Spanish (colonizers, so it's rape, really), and African.

She took care of me the country people way.

For a week afterward, she boiled leaves, threw the hot water in a bucket, and made me sit over it so the steam would go inside me. I didn't believe it would make a difference at first, but clots the size of my fists fell out of me. She massaged my belly with oil and said she had to "put everything back in place." Her exact words. Then she wrapped me with a cloth from under my breasts to my hips to "tie" everything in place so I would get my figure back. The pain was so bad with the wrap on, like I was being cut in half. I cried so much and tried to take it off, but she put the knot at my back and I couldn't undo it.

Now I feel better and my belly stays flat when I take the wrap off to bathe. Only the stretch marks on the lower half of my belly say that I had a child. That and my son. My son. MY SON. Can't believe it. Can't believe that Okonkwo killed the boy when he saw him as a son, and the boy saw Okonkwo as his father.

How could my mother be so distant from me? Stop talking to me when she found out? I don't know her favorite color, song, food. She sent me away but I don't think I can go back. I will go back to Trinidad, but I can't go back to being her daughter in the way I was before. I will be like the narrator in "The Poison Tree," from my poem list.

New Idea #21: I am angry with my mother. When I go back, I will tell her how I feel so at least I can stop feeling this way whenever I think about her. If not, this wrath will grow.

It's been snowing, off and on, since that day at Uncle

Rawle's house. It's really beautiful when it's falling. It slows the world down. After the snow falls, people walking and cars driving mess it up. Then the snow mixes with the dirt and garbage, like someone poured a dirt snow cone everywhere. I put Ike by the window so he could see and know snow even if he doesn't know he knows it yet.

Exercise

I have to start doing sit ups after 40 days, when the belly band comes off.

CXC

- *Reading poems on the syllabus.*

⤶

Spring was rain. The drops as big as pennies sometimes, then fine like a sea spray that Paula couldn't see through the window and had to go outside to feel. Outside, trees were rebuilding their leaves and birds started to appear on the pavement and on the top of the car in the empty lot across the street. Ike slept next to Paula, a pillow on the other side of him, in case he rolled. The nurse in the clinic was concerned that the baby didn't sleep in his own crib and feared that Paula might roll over and crush him. But even in her deepest sleep, Paula knew exactly where that piece of her was and could never destroy it. "It would be like eating and biting off my own finger by mistake," she told the nurse. When Paula asked her aunt about it, she said, "They trying to get you to do things the American way. But sleeping in the same bed with a new baby is our way. By the time you go home, he will be big enough to put in a crib."

By May, the rain had stopped and the trees had completed their fence of leaves. After the baby was born, Paula noticed that her aunt didn't come into her room as often as she used to. When she asked about it, Lorna said that a new mother needed privacy. So Paula was surprised when she came back from a walk with Ike and found Lorna sitting on her bed.

"Something happen?" Paula asked.

Lorna held up an envelope between two fingers. "I buy your ticket." Her voice sounded raspy. "You leaving the twenty-second of May." Lorna read from the ticket. "At am…" She squinted her eyes and moved the ticket farther away from her face. "Four-twenty in the evening. You should—"

"But that is next week."

"I know, but—"

"I talked to Daddy yesterday and, and—you didn't even ask me when I want to go back."

"I know." Lorna closed her eyes. "I know. But this is the best—"

"Best for who? Everybody always know what best for

me. I leaving here just how I come here. They thought it was best and just send me. Now you sending—"

"I will miss you, Paula. This is the best way for me too. I so scared for this room to be empty."

Paula sat next to her and hugged her. Then they talked while she filled a basin with water and wiped off the baby with a wet cloth, dressed him, nursed him, and put him to sleep between the two pillows on the bed. After, she followed her aunt to the kitchen, where they made dinner together and talked some more. Her parents had picked the date and Lorna was glad because she could never have chosen the date that Paula would leave her. Lorna invited her and the baby to visit whenever they wanted. Paula talked about raising the baby without Isaac, about the conversations she wanted to have with her mother, and about applying to UWI after she passed her exams. They speculated about how hot the summer might be and the concerts and outdoor events in Brooklyn where her uncle and aunt might perform.

Later that night, when Paula went to the basement to get the extra suitcases, she thought of how she might never see or do any of the things she talked about with her aunt and was sad. The plans they made, but may not do, were memories that were already fading. As she packed her books and papers, and her and Ike's things, she was happy that she was leaving the next week. The sooner she left, the less she had to lose.

୬

4 June 1996

I didn't see it at the time, but I arrived in the dark so that no one would see me. My mother stayed in the car while Daddy helped with the luggage. When I got to the car, Mummy asked how my flight was, as if I had gone on a holiday. No mention of the baby strapped to my chest. No one asked to hold him. By the time we got to the house, it was after midnight. Perfect.

My room looks exactly the same. I thought they would have put a crib or a cupboard for Ike's things. Whenever I ask for money to go to Marabella or San Fernando to buy things for Ike or myself, Daddy tells me to make a list, and he gets the items. He wouldn't even let me go for the drive with him.

When my parents are at work, I watch TV in the drawing room and play with the baby. When they are home, I stay in my room. Kind of afraid. Not knowing how to start a conversation after so much distance. I had planned to have all these talks and say all this stuff. I was brave from afar but far from brave.

⤦

In Trinidad, June, the start of the wet season, brought humid nights and days. Her parents' concrete house, with its slivers of clay ventilation blocks above each window, was hot and uncomfortable. Paula wanted to go outside, but Ike was asleep on the bed next to her. She pulled the button on the fan so it stopped oscillating and sent air directly onto her and the baby. From the bedroom, the fridge's motor tripped in and out, and the bottles on top of the fridge vibrated with the hum. She sucked her teeth, glanced at her son, and went to the kitchen to separate the two or more bottles that made the tinny rattle. As she made her way back, she heard a metallic click at the front of the house, then the rumble of the wrought-iron gate sliding toward the wall to let her father's car into the garage. She returned to the kitchen and opened the fridge so her parents might find her there, to create a situation where they might talk. Car doors closed under the house, and she remembered Ike dammed only by soft pillows and went back to the room.

Her parents talked as they entered the house, then, like most evenings, the sounds disappeared into the bedroom down the hall. Footfalls approached her door. A knock.

"Yes." Paula sat up.

Her mother opened the door and leaned against the wall with both hands behind her back. "Is time for you to return to your life." She had cut her hair, which made her head look smaller and emphasized the weight she'd lost. "You don't have to mind this child, you know. You could have a life—"

"Who will mind it, if not me?"

"I. Me. It will be my child, and you can go on with your life."

"Your child? I knew this all along, you know. You want me to pretend that my son is my brother and we all pretend like nothing happen? Like some rich people trying to hide incest or something?"

"You don't have to be so vulgar. And you don't have to raise your voice. This is what is going to happen."

"No."

"No? What you mean no? You don't have a choice. This is my house and you are my daughter and you will live like I say to live."

"No. I don't want that. I want to go back to school, go to UWI, and get a job and take care of Ikemefuna, for myself."

"Stop it with that foolish name." She covered her ears. "He will be Anthony Benedict, after the saints for the twelfth of January. And you can't do those things with a child in tow. You need help and the only way I going to help you is by taking the child." She sat next to her daughter. "I'm saving your reputation, child. Nobody would want you if they knew about this. Nobody would hire—"

"Yes, they will. I am not ashamed. This is about *your* reputation. I don't care what people think about me."

"I got the nuns to agree to let you come back. And I will get you into UWI. A job. You can't do these things on your own."

"I can't do things in the way you want. But I can do other things, my way." Paula stood and folded her arms.

"What you mean by that?"

Ike twisted against the pillow. For a moment, both mother and daughter looked at him.

"I will lock you in this house if I have to. I will lock you in this room until you get some sense."

Her mother waited a few seconds then walked out. Moments later, the corridor shivered as her mother slammed the bedroom door down the hall. Paula could just make out the contours of a high-pitched voice as her mother complained to her father, Okonkwo's silent wife, but couldn't catch all the words.

✍

5 June 1996

This morning when I got up, I expected the room door to be locked from the outside, but it wasn't. Her and Daddy went to work as normal. I called I.'s mother and told her about the whole situation. She wanted to see her grandson.

I. didn't even tell her. What does that mean? I need to think more about this.

I called my friends from school and told them. Lorraine, then Nalini and Sasha. Sasha talks a lot and will tell everybody, even if she promised me to not tell people.

I called the secretary of the Lions Club and told her.

*I called Daddy at work and asked if he would help
me pay for a babysitter, sign me up for school and give
me money to get things done. He sighed and breathed
like he does when he's thinking then asked me if it was
what I wanted. I said yes and he said he would do it.
Then he asked: What about your mother?*

And I asked: What about my father?

Then Okonkwo's wife said okay.

*I called a few of the senior secondary schools and
made an appointment with two principals, for me
and Daddy to talk about a place to sit exams next
January. They were not prestige Catholic schools. I
went to one and look how I turned out. (Laugh.)
I am proof that prestige and donations and dinner
with the bishop don't matter.*

*I wonder if Auntie knew about Mummy taking the
baby all along. I tried to remember that conversation
we had after my first week. Was there a pause or a
look? I re-read the journal and couldn't find anything.*

*New Idea #33: When she calls next time, ask Auntie
if she knew about the plan all along. If she didn't
know, ask her for advice. Ask her to send money
by Western Union. Walk to the lotto place at the
junction to collect it.*

After my phone calls today, I got dressed and went out. It was midday and the sun was real hot, beating down on me and poor Ike. I went back to the house and waited till after two o'clock, when it was cooler, and went out again. Mrs. Montoute was watering her plants in her front yard. I went right up to the gate and said hello. I let her hold Ike and told her he was mine. I could see other questions forming in her eyes, but she didn't ask them. She kept saying how nice the baby was and cooed at him.

After Mrs. Montoute, I walked out onto the main road and said hello to everyone I met and introduced my son to anyone that my parents talked to. By the end of the day, I was no longer a secret. If Mummy did lock me in the house, people might ask for me.

Exercise

60 sit ups

60 leg lifts (30 per leg)

Walk around the neighborhood.

CXC

- *Ask Daddy if he could sign me up for lessons. I need more practice to make sure I pass my exams on the first try.*

- *I need more practice being with other people besides my parents.*
- *Everything depends on it.*

"I know how to get him to give yuh de money.
Remember ole fire stick easy to ketch."

– CANDACE, 2014

Ready for the Revolution?

OUT OF THE blue Tricia texted me:

Hey. Have issues with

men. With the few

opps that exist for blks.

Sry for dissing your diss

+ pulling you into a fight.

What you said had me

🔥*. I said some* 🔥 *stuff*

too. Idk what to say/do

at this point

I'd called twice before her text. Had apologized in a voicemail the first time. Then hung up when she didn't pick up the second time. After that, nothing between us. Until, three months later, I saw her at the Graduate Center Library and, just to see what would happen, I sat across from her. She looked drawn. Thinner? She didn't look up when I said hello.

"I got your text." Get right to it.

"So you know how I feel then." She turned a page in her book. "The police thing was a crazy thing to say, Darren."

I shrugged.

"Nothing?" She looked at me now.

I waited for the moment to pass. Saying sorry was always hard for me. We were on the second floor of the library, near the windows overlooking 35th Street. It was late March and sunlight hit her books, the desk, her face and made a star that orbited the arc of her lower lip.

"Sorry."

She nodded then looked out the window then back at me. The desk shook as she tapped one foot underneath, one of her few things-that-could-annoy-but-didn't habits.

"I am." I took out my laptop and we worked in silence. Usually, I would be winding down with a Hole of Convenience (HoC) by this time of year, but everything was different with Tricia.

After two hours or so, she declared she was taking

a break. We went to the dingy room with tables and armchairs next to the café and talked like before, only her laughs and smiles were hesitant and nervous. As we left the library later that day, I asked, "Want to go for a drink?" My department was sponsoring a thing for a visiting professor at a restaurant nearby.

"I'd planned to go straight home. I need another layer." She lifted her shoulders and hugged herself. When she accepted the gray sweater I always carried in my bag, I felt like she was also accepting my sorry.

The private room at the back of the restaurant was dimly lit, filled with murmuring voices and the sharp kisses between cutlery and porcelain. As I shook hands and chatted with the guest of honor from Tanzania, a specialist on Asian merchants in the British Colonial Empire, Tricia mingled. My body clocked hers as she circled between jeaned and hoodied students and white-haired faculty. That night, both of us drunk on too-dry wine, we walked along 34th Street and joked about the way this tall skinny guy, who we could see wherever we went in the room, was trying to ingratiate himself to the colonial scholar to get him on his dissertation committee.

"Right there in front of everyone," she yelled. "It was like academic porn."

"No! Dissertation porn."

She shrieked then covered her mouth.

I wanted to kiss her but stopped a few inches from her face, wary of the past.

She kissed me. Quick. Like she was trying it out to see what would happen.

"I'll see you next time." That wasn't what I meant to say. The wine delayed my reaction to the kiss, so my mouth uttered what I was planning to say before she did it.

"You can see me now."

~

The next morning, I sat in bed with both knees drawn up and the white covers between my legs made them look like hills rimmed with cloud.

"I thought you were celibate?"

"Was." She put her chin on my shoulder like we'd always done this. "Until two weeks ago."

"Awright." I tried to picture the man who she could have met and been with in only two months when she had refused me for three.

"My ex."

Outside, cars made slushy sounds as they drove on roads wet from rain mixed with snow that had fallen earlier that morning. These sounds made our conversation seem domestic and routine. I had to be in Trinidad before the summer to complete my interviews and look for documents. Her HoC status was coming to an end. And maybe I was mad about the celibacy thing. Yeah. I was.

"Now, Miss Tricia Morrell, I have to go. Do some writing."

"Now?" She reached under the covers. I shifted my hips so she'd miss her mark. She sat up. Breasts flopped against her chest.

I kissed her in the space between her nose and upper lip and sprang off the bed.

"Am I going to be doing the walk of shame by myself?" she asked.

"Um…" I stretched my arms above my head and smelled my armpits. Sour. "I'm not that kinda fella."

"What kinda fella are you?"

I laughed because I didn't know what to say.

She moved the curtain of hair from her eyes and looked at me. No. *Saw me*, I realized, months later.

❧

We'd met the October before, at a seminar on activism at the Graduate Center. During the Q&A, she asked if Black Lives Matter was still a genuine movement, not co-opted by capitalism and the media.

There was a murmur. A clap started that was picked up by a few, then a few more, until the whole room was clapping. Tomkins, a policy guy from one of the public colleges, said something about BLM being co-opted by armchair and social media activists who wore BLM T-shirts and put signs in their windows but had never waved a banner, signed a petition, or been in a sit-in. It was "activism"—he made air quotes—without ever leaving the comfort of your home or taking your eyes from your smart phone.

After that, a man asked another BLM question, and for the rest of the Q&A the conversation centered around BLM and the role of activism under the Obama presidency. I was hoping to ask a question about connections between Black Power in Trinidad in the 1960s and '70s and the resurgence of militant activism in the United States. When the Q&A was over, I went on stage and posed my question to Tomkins, who saw a connection and suggested a book and some papers that were probably at Howard University. Tricia was still on stage, shaking hands and smiling. A few of the all-male white panel, confounded by her luminous eyes and Grace Jones body, seemed to bow as they shook her hand. (Whose idea was it to have a panel on activism with no women, no people of color, and nobody outside of academia?) When the stage cleared, I introduced myself and walked out with her.

Tricia, a doctoral student in American Studies at New York University who was taking two courses at the GC, said she liked my accent, so I brought out the full Trini to make her laugh. I couldn't tell if she liked me, the minimum requirement for a HoC. I walked her to the F-train and took the number 2, but didn't think about her that night, and not for a while anyhow, because the diss wasn't going so well.

The next day, a bird singing outside my apartment window seemed to be keeping pace with Lord Invader's voice on my CD player. The calypsonian's lyrics mentioned rivalry between political parties and

Black Power but there was nothing to support my idea that events and race relations in Trinidad in the 1940s shaped Stokely Carmichael/Kwame Touré's activism in the States. I opened the window to look for the little singer in the tree outside on Nostrand Avenue. At the same moment, a truck horn blared and the bird, a fan of brown feathers, flew away. I kept the window open as I worked on Chapter Four: Race Relations in the First Eleven Years, so that the car noises and voices that made it up to the third floor became the soundtrack to my writing. I wrote till four o' clock, taught my Intro to Caribbean and Latin American History class at Brooklyn College, then met Hugh for our regular.

For the first half hour, like he did every time we met, Hugh talked about his graduate fieldwork in Africa and about Kwesi, the "wonderful young man" from Sierra Leone "who could have been a star" had he lived. After the second Kwesi story, I offered to send my first three chapters to him. "To see if it's on track."

"Nah." Hugh waved his fat hands and pointy fingers without taking his elbows off the arms of his chair. "Just give it to me when you're done."

A crease appeared between his eyes so I smiled to break up my face, which, to him must have looked like an impenetrable stone. "Okay." I stood, my back bent a little so I wouldn't look too tall in his small, bare office. "When ah done den." Everyone gets angry in their native tongue.

"Listen," he said as he got up. His gray, cashmered

belly jutted out at me. "If you were any other student, I would look at every chapter. But you're very bright. And a good writer. I wish all my graduate students were like you. Hell, you should've been a woman. Then we could check off two boxes on those EOC compliance things." He slapped me on the shoulder. "Ha, ha, ha."

I laughed too. But I wanted to argue, insist he read the draft, use words like *fock* and *muddah cunt* and pound on the table and...and other words that faded as I crossed the empty campus with its tall bright lamps that had chastened the dark and my mood by the time I'd exited through the south gate.

∽

November's cold air quieted Nostrand, as the mostly Caribbean residents didn't linger on the street. The quiet outside was like some big spongy thing trying to force its way into my apartment, making the pre-war one-bedroom seem smaller. Me and my books and papers were too big for the place, so I started writing at the GC library.

One evening, a month or so after meeting her at the GC auditorium, I found Tricia on the second floor bracketed by two piles of books. I walked over and said hey.

For a few seconds, a curve formed between her eyes, then she smiled.

"Hey yourself, Trini." She was working on her proposal but wouldn't tell me what it was about. Didn't matter. From then on, whenever I was at the GC, we took breaks together in the grimy lounge next to the library or in the Starbucks on 35th. At first, we talked about Stokely and Black Power, then the convo switched to the economic situation for Blacks after slavery in the U.S. Her proposal topic, I realized later. We wrote in the same building and talked while we ate, but didn't get closer until a few weeks into our routine when she took me to Zara.

I followed her around the store while she browsed and tried things on. Women and girls crisscrossed the store and filled it with excited talk and the sounds of hangers gliding along metal racks. Every now and then, Tricia would appear at the changing room door in minis and other tight things. Without looking at me, she commented on how fat her thighs were or how something made her look old. And I, like a chupidee, smiled and refuted every claim, then wondered if I'd bowed to her beauty like the men on the panel had almost three months earlier. A Zara run was a boyfriend thing. A couple's thing. I didn't realize I was annoyed until, just before she ran down the subway steps, I held her arm.

"What?"

"You have a man? What we doing here?"

Her heart-shaped lips grinned.

"I serious. What we doing?" I let her go.

"I'm celibate, Darren."

I pretended not to hear it. "I like you, Tricia. You know that. I want to be your man." I had to try a thing.

"But I'm celibate. It won't be much fun for you." The pink lights from Victoria's Secret twinkled in her eyes. "And I know how you island men are. All that hot sun in your blood—"

"Stop right there!" I explained that her celibacy didn't mean we couldn't date. Normally, I didn't date my HoCs, but, like I said, this whole thing was happening in a different way. Then, I went ivory tower and said she had a simplified, prejudiced view of Caribbean men, and other overused tropes from the identity politics playbook. It worked, because she apologized and agreed to dinner that weekend. As soon as Tricia had descended the subway stairs, I called a former HoC from a year ago. She was home and said I could come over and watch Netflix and eat Chinese food with her. After the call, I waited ten minutes to be sure that Tricia was well on her way to Queens. I was still looking around for her when I boarded the F to Brooklyn. By Second Avenue, I felt at ease and was already thinking of the route I'd take from _____'s apartment on the walk of shame the next day.

◈

My first date with Tricia went fine. Food, nuanced academic talk, and a fraternal hug at the train station before she descended the steps. On the third date, around Christmas, at an Indian restaurant near Astor Place, I told her about my fellowship with tuition and a stipend.

"You know you're benefiting from affirmative

action, right?" She dropped the spoon in the copper bowl and tikka sauce splashed across the table.

"I'm benefiting from hard work and late nights. I deserve it."

"Deserve? Your grandparents didn't march. Get mauled by police dogs. Nobody opened a fire hydrant on them. We fought for this. And we continue to not get our share. Because Caribbean people displace us as the preferred kind of Black. I see you nodding hello at the cops you know—"

"And don't forget Mutumbu an' dem." I grinned, then pretended to blow a dart through a hole in my fist.

"This isn't funny, Darren. Yes, Africans too. Black with European sensibilities. Exotic because they have real 'traditions'"—she made air quotations—"that Whites could see. Better than former slaves. You getting a fellowship meant for African Americans is like a theft. And one day you—and Mutumbu"—she made her voice deeper to mock me—"will have to make reparations."

I mentioned Stokely and his activism with Martin Luther King and the Black Panthers.

"Stokely was a sellout. A dictator. When King and everybody wanted a peaceful movement. For policy. Lasting change. He didn't and went to Africa and had hisself a Black Power movement all by hisself." She held up a Black Power fist then spread her fingers so it exploded.

I was about to say how King had divided the movement, but couldn't get a word in.

"And Stokely. One guy. Isn't enough to pay the way for all of you." Her lips got thin and flat.

"I don't think anyone," I said slowly, "especially a fellowship committee, makes the distinction between one kind of Black person and another." I hoped to salvage the date and get back to my biryani. But she goaded me. Talked shit about Stokely and called my diss an apology. While she talked, I had the urge to kiss her lips. No, I wanted to bite them then swallow her whole. I felt weird, and suddenly I couldn't hear what she was saying and had no sense of time or where I was in relation to the rest of the world. It was just her, my erection, and a thumping sound in both ears.

She hit the table with her palms and the dishes jumped, a metallic rattle. "What? Cat got your tongue?"

I closed my eyes, then opened them. Tricia was looking at me. And checking me out, I think.

"I wish your cat would allow my tongue." I leaned back and looked directly into her eyes.

She stared back and I thought I saw her heart beating fast at the base of her fine neck. A short quick breath moved between her parted lips.

She refused me. With some feminist, existential explanation that made any arousal a form of assault. A door inside me swung open and words poured out. I told her that American-born Blacks (*You People!* is what I said) dropped out of doctoral programs like flies because they expected everything to be handed to them. Then I felt free, didn't give a fock because I'd been following her around for three months, reading articles not on my reading list so I could have convos with her, and dealing a former HoC on the side to get by, and said, "Dat is why de police always shooting allyuh."

She stood. The dishes jangled on the table. She picked up her coat and walked out.

The thumping in my ears subsided and I was back in the world again. The smell of cardamom rose from the biryani, and I felt the chair against my shoulder blades and along my spine. I paid the bill and walked through Lower Manhattan, along the Bowery and across the Brooklyn Bridge. The carpet of lights below me, the breeze blowing up from the water, couples holding hands and tourists posing for pictures, made the walk seem otherworldly. By the time I descended the steps to Washington Street, the conversation and the unfinished meal seemed to have happened a lifetime ago.

❧

Our first night together was nearly five months after the activism seminar. Guess we got there, and once we did, we were a regular thing. We slept at each other's apartment and met at the GC to write and talk. As May ended, I prepared to go to Trinidad. I sublet the apartment to a student from Bolivia, who had a violin fellowship at Carnegie Hall. I had planned that, before I left, I would treat Tricia to the MO I used when I wanted to discharge an HoC—answer every other call then every two and so on, refuse opportunities for sex, and, when I did see her, let her do all the talking. But, before I could start break-up proceedings, Tricia left for North Carolina to begin research for her diss. She sent me an email a day after she arrived. We was by my apartment two nights before and she never say a friggin' word. When I read dat email eh…meh body geh weak. Like I was *she* Pole ah Convenience and *she* was slacking me off as part a *she* MO. I didn't email she back. Stchuuu.

While I waited to board the plane to Port-of-Spain, I kept checking my phone for a message that could provide an opportunity to regain my position as the king of the little republic we had. Nothing. I took the sim card out when my group was called. On the plastic-encased path to the plane door, I took off New York, grad school, Tricia, everything, like a jacket. Only the diss stayed with me, as close as my ribs.

⁓

I got to the Scheme in South Trinidad at night. Ma, who everyone called Miss Nursey because she was a nurse at San Fernando General Hospital, cried and held me tight. She was warm and smelled of White Satin perfume. I wanted to rest my head against her belly like when I was a boy so that her warmth and scent could crowd out all the thoughts in my head.

The Scheme, short for Government Housing Scheme, was built in the 1970s as part of a government project to house squatters and others in urban areas, largely Afro-Trinidadians, who couldn't afford housing. Early the next day, a Sunday, we caught an around-the-town car at the Scheme entrance and went to the market on Mucurapo Street. The market was mostly unchanged, a large open concrete shed, just off the street, that smelled like onions and smoked herring. What had changed was that some vendors sold cell phone cases, chargers, and headphones, along with vegetables and meat. Outside, there were vendors selling things like aloo pies, doubles, and burgers from the backs of trucks and metal kiosks with full color screen-printed graphics of shiny fries and cans of Coca Cola with perfect beads of water on them. These carts could be in any city in the world. Some vendors, like Miss Millie, who was now blind in one eye, remembered me and talked about when I used to haggle for the lowest price just before the market closed. As we left those stalls, vendors threw a little extra of what we had already bought into our woven plastic shopping bag, handfuls of homecoming to show they were glad to see me.

When we got home, Ma cooked my favorites—stewed chicken, macaroni pie, and fried rice with a lettuce and cucumber salad. She watched as I ate at the kitchen table, where she still kept a red-and-white plaid plastic tablecloth, with matching salt and pepper shakers on either side of a napkin holder, like a table in a restaurant, expecting customers any minute.

"You get so small. What you do for food when you up there?" She asked this same question when I called her from New York.

"I buy it or cook sometimes." Her hair had grayed at the front and her cheekbones protruded slightly. "You awright, Ma? You get small too."

"You know…" She shrugged. "No rest for the wicked. You want me to tell people you come? Or you here to study?"

"I here to study." I put a spoonful in my mouth and chewed. "You remember the long, long paper I tell you about? To finish the degree?"

She nodded.

"Well, I want to finish it by August. So I go be writing real plenty. Sometimes I might have to go to the University of the West Indies or to talk to some people…"

"And then you will be a professor?" She put a piece of lettuce back on my plate that had fallen onto the table.

"Yeah." It was easier than the truth.

She clapped her hands above her head. "Darren, if you know how I does pray for you." She put her clasped hands between her thighs and smiled.

I leaned in so I could be closer to her. "You sure you not hungry? Is nearly one o'clock."

She narrowed her eyes and looked up.

"What?" I asked.

"I checking to see if I hungry."

We both laughed.

"Yes. I'll take a lil' thing. Just rice and gravy and salad."

I made her a plate.

The outside walls of the housing blocks in the Scheme were a faded orange with splashes of dirt and dust close to the ground, like a shadow hedge. Many of the families I had known still lived in the blocks in some form; either the parents had died and left adult children or the families had moved out and the apartment was occupied by relatives new to San Fernando. I stayed inside for the first two weeks, sorting papers and making appointments for interviews. Other than the sound of cars passing on the street and the occasional dog or radio, there was a lulling quiet that was only interrupted by the sound of Ma's key in the door after her shift.

I stopped working when she was there. Then, I'd watch her cook dinner while we talked about New York, and President Obama and his family. Then we'd switch to talking about Trinidad politics. She hated all the political parties and thought that the People's National Movement, the party she once voted for, "didn't keep its promise to Trini people," and the "PNM thief all the money." I didn't agree with her, but didn't say so to avoid being *that son*. That son who got a little education and thought his mother didn't know anything anymore.

Once I started my research, I left early in the

morning and came back just before Ma did. Somehow, people still found out I was home and sent messages through Ma. The first was Nigel Harris, who I had gone to secondary school with. I was at home, listening to recorded interviews, when he knocked on the door one weekday afternoon. I peeped through the living room curtain to see who it was.

"Open de door nah man," Nigel shouted.

He grabbed me in a rough hug. "Darko! Long time. How you doing, man?"

I had forgotten about the nickname. In secondary, I was Darko in our set of four dark-skinned friends who used to lime together. Nigel was Blue Black. Lyndon Mobsey, Black Boy, and Colin Hunt, the darkest of us, was the Ace of Spades.

"Nigel. I good. Cool."

"I is Blue. You forget?"

"I remember. You look good though." His belly hung over his large silver-colored belt buckle. The hairy eye of his navel looked out at me from under the curve of his faded gray polo shirt.

"You looking real good. Still in shape."

"All them is yours?" I pointed at the children with him.

"Yeah. Come." Nigel pushed them forward. "This is the oldest, Kerron, he eight. Nobel, five, and this is the queen." He lifted a thin girl with two long braids into his arms. "Maya, four. Ent Maya, you is the queen?" He rubbed his nose into her chest.

"Yes!" she said and we laughed.

"You want to come in?" I offered.

"Nah, can't stay. They have to change and reach karate class for five. So, everything awright with you? You here to stay? Visit?"

"Visit. Here to finish up some things for school."

"I hear 'bout that. Miss Nursey tell me. Still a scholar. You was always the brightest one. Me, I working in a mechanic's place in Pleasantville. Married to Sasha."

"I hear so." I pictured Sasha in her plaid pleated skirt and matching tie, her hair in two long plaits, just like Maya's.

"Yeah. Five years now. We live in the blocks. 2H. Second Hibiscus Block. Right where my mother used to live. You know she die, right?"

I did know.

"Cancer. Yeah. It was rough. You must come through for a lime before you go back. When you going?"

"September." I didn't want to be back in secondary school again, like a pair of training wheels rolling behind Blue and Sasha as they ran away to the beach. Other times, walking between them to create the illusion that Blue and Sasha were just friends.

"Okay, so we have time to link. Have to go. Go check yuh."

❧

Dexter Mitchell, Candice's brother, was more persistent. He invited himself in one evening, then

A. K. Herman

knocked on our door almost every night for a week just after Ma got home to invite me for a lime. Candice was the first girl I was with, and I thought I was going to marry her. I also thought Dexter would have plenty people, food, and drinks, but when I got there, it was just Dexter, a half-bottle of warm white rum, and two glasses. We talked about politics and Dexter's job as a P.E. teacher, then Dexter asked me for money. I told him I didn't have any and he accused me of returning to Trinidad to "show off on poor people." Then, embarrassed, he changed the subject and fingered the glass for long stretches between words. I hung around for an hour and made jokes about it. After that night, we waved quickly and didn't stop to talk when we encountered each other in the Scheme.

The same week, Candice showed up. When Ma got up to refill her glass of sorrel, she put her foot on my crotch under the kitchen table. I started talking about the girlfriend I had in New York.

"True?" Candice asked.

Ma poured the sorrel and sat down.

"She studying at NYU. Right now, she in North Carolina working on she studies, while I doing mine here." That morning, Tricia had emailed to say her research was going well and asked about mine.

No. I didn't answer any of she emails.

Yes. Still vex 'bout allegedly. Me being she PoC.

Still, as I talked about her to Candice, Tricia seemed

102

more real and vivid to me than the person who sent the email.

"Hmm. That is nice." Candice withdrew her foot.

Afterward, Ma asked about Tricia.

"I only say that to put Candice off the scent."

She raised an eyebrow.

"First the brother come sniffing, now Candice." Not sure what Ma thought about that, but she didn't say more.

✑

When I wasn't at UWI selecting documents to copy or interviewing the remnants of Trinidad's revolutionaries, men who still wore jackets with mandarin collars and didn't trim their beards, I wrote one thousand to fifteen hundred words a day. It came up in a few interviews that I should talk to more people in Grenada, but I had already spent a summer there and I wanted to be done. By July, I had a clarity about the diss that had eluded me in New York. It was as if what the research had to say about the social climate that shaped Stokely's activism could only be heard, felt in this place. Other things occurred to me too. The jacket I had taken off when I boarded the plane to Port-of-Spain was replaced by another as whatever status people thought I had by spending nine years in the States had blown away like sugarcane ash in the wind. In Trinidad, I was like everybody else, nothing exceptional. Here, everybody wore the same jacket and didn't seem to notice it or the jacket of people around them. I felt the fabric of Trinidad against my back and chest and, sometimes, the tag at the back of the collar irritated the nape of my neck.

❧

Once I was back in New York, I put in my sim card and found four text messages from Tricia. In the first two, she talked about her research. In the others, she had finished her interviews and was wondering if I was still in Trinidad and if she could fly over. I started to text her back but couldn't finish it. The morning I left, Ma stayed in her room so she wouldn't see me walking through the door with my luggage, my back to her. Not seeing her before I left and returning to the empty apartment that my sublet had left pristine made me feel unmoored, not connected to anything. I called Tricia.

"Hi, Darren," she said and laughed an easy laugh. We made a dinner date for later that night as she was excited to hear about my process for completing a draft of the diss: "Ready for the Revolution?": How the racial politics of Trinidad (1939 to 1952) shaped Stokely Carmichael/Kwame Touré's activism.

❧

In the small office in the history department at Brooklyn College, Hugh was furious.

"It's too political. Too much like Carmichael himself. A divisive figure in American activism. But you know this, Darren." He drew the tips of his fingers together like a teepee then spread them wide. "You know all of this—"

"The work, including the title, should reflect who Carmichael/Touré was. He answered the phone with this question until he died." I tapped my pen on the edge of the table.

"No. This work is about how a society influenced Carmichael's progressive ideas about Blackness in the American activist landscape. This title"—his fingers tented again—"is a daytime talk show. A provocateur. Not fitting for— Please, I can't think with that noise."

I tapped the pen against my thigh.

"Not fitting for an academic work in a history department. This isn't what I expected of you. Your work should draw people in. Not stop them at the gates. This is exactly what Carmichael wanted to do. I cannot move forward with this title."

I kept the subtitle only and defended the diss with Hugh and two other committee members.

Pass with minor revisions.

The next day, Hugh took me to lunch and, as I strutted in a new suit from the French bistro on 36th and Fifth, I realized I wanted to celebrate even more. I called Ma, who cried and prayed with me. Then I flicked through my phone contacts, browsing the names of people from undergrad and a few people who I'd connected with when I started the doctoral program. Both groups had receded to the periphery of my research, teaching and writing. So, I went dancing and drinking with you know who. Everything she said was funny. Or I was real drunk.

It was a warmish September night and vendors were still out on the sidewalk near my apartment building. The dread who sold incense called out to me, "Soldier."

"Brethren," I answered.

We walked to his one-table stall. The bottles of oil on the table were amber-colored and wavered under the streetlight like a dream happening in Brooklyn.

"Miss?" He held up some incense sticks for Tricia to smell. "Damask rose. Mi 'ave Chanel too. Want smell it?"

"How much is this one?"

"Five fi di rose. Twenty inna di pack."

She paid and took the bag.

"She 'ave good tase," he said to me.

It sounded like an approval.

She introduced herself.

"Titus Carrington." He touched his chest.

She asked if he made a good living selling on the street and they started to talk about the changes in the neighborhood and the weather. I wanted to pee and said so. They quieted their talk and I linked my arm in hers until we were in front of my apartment door. As she opened the door, I muttered thank you and she hugged me to her. I was thanking her for being there, for buying incense from a Rasta man on the street and treating him like he was at a perfume counter in a fancy department store. I didn't know what her hug meant.

❧

The following January, I got a job as a lecturer in the history department. To get Tricia closer— yes, indeed, so I may begin formerly truncated break-up proceedings—I took her to dinners, gave her pointers on her writing, and sometimes spent the weekend at her place in Jackson Heights. She changed. She stopped laughing all the time and openly disagreed with me in long discussions about history, race, and colonialism. I loved our disagreements best. The day after I announced I was going to turn the diss into a book, she brought me a thousand index cards and Post-it Notes to *organize your thoughts. See the book.* I felt so close to her at that moment I put the cards and Post-its on my desk and made love to her as if it was the first time, enjoying each shapely limb and prolonging her pleasure as long as I could.

Afterward, I watched her sleep. There was no movement under her eyelids. There was no rise and fall of her body. I thought that she'd died. In a panic, I knelt on the bed, shook her shoulders and called her name, my voice breathy and shaking.

"You awright?" I asked when she opened her eyes.

"Better than alright." She smiled and hugged my neck with both arms.

That is how love happens. You panic at the thought of her dying. I felt my heart slow.

"I know what kind of guy you are now," she said

against my ear. Then she looked at me the same way she did after our first night together, only her gaze was softer, like I'd stolen something unimportant and was found out.

When Ma came for the graduation ceremony in June, I introduced Tricia as my girlfriend. I watched to see if she was surprised, but she hugged Ma and didn't even look at me. After the introduction, Ma clapped her hands and looked up at the sky.

"I so happy to meet you. He hardly talk about any girls."

❧

For the book, I used the original title and the publishers, a small university press, loved it. Hugh wrote the introduction and, in it, said that the book was *timely, a love letter to the BLM Movement*, the title *fitting*.

Imagine? Focking FITTING!

After the book came out, I accepted an assistant professor position that began the following fall. The position, orchestrated by Hugh, was in history but almost all my courses were cross-listed with Caribbean Studies and Africana Studies. I taught two American History courses, but that wasn't enough to stop a bald, jeans-wearing, corduroy-patches-on-the-elbows-of-his-jacket colleague from telling me in the bathroom: "You're really in Caribbean Studies. But they didn't have a line. And we really needed a Black guy, so we're footing the bill."

I'd already figured this out, but hearing it just before my class made me feel sad then vexed and, by the time I walked into the classroom, I was too confused to deliver my lecture, so I gave the students an assignment and left for the day.

Two years into my new position, Hugh knocked on the door of my office and sat down. He asked about Tricia and joked about students not doing their reading assignments. Then he asked if I was working on anything.

"Just editing a paper for a journal." I paused. "And thinking about a new book. Something about activism in Eric Williams's writings. Don't really know yet."

"Hmm…" Hugh began. "That could be your third book. How about you and I write a book together?"

I waited for more.

"On worker activism in Sierra Leone in the 1970s."

"Africa's not really my area—"

"Africa. Caribbean. It's all the same to these people." He waved his hands in a circle to point to the whole department. "Hey," he whispered. "I'm going to be honest with you. I'm a middle-aged White guy. You're an up-and-coming Black guy. I have license to write about activism. But not about Black activism, let alone African activism. Especially with all that's been going on. Lives mattering and all that. You're one of the most capable people I know. Not like these pretending assholes in the department who got tenure in the '80s and haven't done anything since, except maybe vote in union elections to make sure their salary increases pass."

You need me for legitimacy, I thought.

"And it will look great for the tenure committee that you've collaborated with"—Hugh smiled then folded his arms across his chest—"a senior colleague."

Quid pro focking quo. The thought must have showed on my face because Hugh touched my hand and said, "I'm sorry. I didn't mean that to sound like quid pro quo because of the job and everything. It's just that this project will bridge…"

I stopped listening.

When Hugh was finished, I told him I'd think about it and went home.

Back in the apartment, Tricia's red fleece hoodie greeted me from the back of the chair at the desk in the living room. She was supposed to come by after her class, so I took two burgers from the freezer to thaw. As I washed the lettuce and sliced the tomatoes, I wondered if I could find another position somewhere else, somewhere where I wasn't a stepchild. There was a university in Florida with a strong Caribbean and Latin American Department, but I was afraid to start the tenure clock from scratch again. I could go back to Trinidad, teach at UWI, be a lecturer my whole career. And Tricia was still working on her diss and would probably take the same path I did;

get a lecturer position at NYU where she was now an adjunct, her diss chair would groom her for the first assistant professorship that opened up.

It was almost eight o'clock. Tricia was supposed to arrive in a few minutes and I didn't want my conversation with Hugh to hang in the apartment like a bad smell, so I emailed him my decision:

Hugh,

Yes. I will work on the project with you. I've been thinking about ways to expand my scholarship beyond the Caribbean region and this is just the way to do it. I appreciate you asking me. ☺

Let's talk tomorrow about next steps—writing a proposal for funding, applying for leave, etc. Don't hesitate to ask if you need anything from me to move forward on this.

Best,

Darren

D. Baker, Ph.D.

Assistant Professor of History

Brooklyn College

Department of History

1560 Bedford Avenue, Rm 113

Brooklyn, NY 11201

(718) 981-2700

bakerd@brooklyncollege.edu

@fittingtrini

"Who really is this Darko?"- Unknown

"I follow Hector eyes to he laugh lines, he neck and the blocky shoulders that make me look at him more than anybody who psssst at me when I walking in town."

— Queenie, 1946

Love

WHEN THE LAST shudder passed through me, I got up from Leo. Without talking, because we never talked afterwards, he rested his head on the folded rice bag and stared up at the ceiling of the bush house. I opened the door and went by the river to wash myself, not wanting to spend the rest of the day with between my legs feeling slippery, slippery. The water was cool, the morning too for that matter. As I squatted down, my cotton dress disturbed the dew on some Shame Charlottes and other low plants at the riverbank. The Shame Charlottes's leaves closed, like little hands in prayer, as the cotton touched them. All of a sudden, birds darted from the trees overlooking the river. Two signs? If I told Leo, he will fly from me just as the birds flew from the trees and I will need to hide my face like the shameful plant? Or I ought to be thankful, my hands in prayer, as what we have together will take flight?

By the time I had returned to the bush house, he was up and dressed, with his walking stick in one hand and a thick cow rope in the other. Before I could say anything, a cow in the distance bellowed, like a person calling a name. Leo looked in the direction of the noise and not at me. They need pasture, he said. They calling for me.

This man and his animals, eh. He talks to them, hears them talking back. But each one of those cows is destined for the abattoir some Friday. I went right up to his face and called his name in a whisper like I do when we were about to get to the top of our mountain and he gripped my hips to stay on earth a little longer.

He turned toward me and smiled.

We will take flight. There will be no shame today.

His face was so perfect. Straight nose. Good soil on his head. A tall slim-body man.

Betty. They calling. He squeezed my left shoulder like I was a man-friend in a rum shop and he had just bought a round of drinks but couldn't stay.

Leo. I put my hand on my stomach. I am pregnant.

He dropped the rope, then staggered back like I had pushed him.

Wha' yuh ah sey?

The grove was quiet. The trees and low plants waited. Only the river splush-sploshed in the distance as it carried away our natures, mixed together.

You heard what I said, my lover. I am three months.

The cows called in the distance and he looked in the direction of the sound.

I backed away from him. What is the matter, Leo? We've been turning turtle for months now. You and I. What is it?

I don't know, Betty.

What you don't know?

I don't know what we going to do. Well, he looked up, Ann making a baby too.

The sliding block puzzle of my thoughts moved round, and made a scraping sound, until everything made sense. The other day, I noticed Ann in town and she had put on a little weight at her middle. A heaviness in her chest. A brightness in her face.

I touched his cheek, the same color as my hand. We are a match. Complexion. We look at the world the same way. I have the womanhood to match his manhood. A match.

A vexation was rising in me, like an agouti pacing in a cage, because he was talking about Ann when I was telling him about our child. So, I put my voice soft so I will sound tender, like a new leaf on a corn stalk. What, love?

It's getting late and you need to get to work. Leh ah we talk 'bout dis later, nuh?

He started to talk bad, like a man from the village, which meant his mind was already gone from here. From me.

Alright, I said. The 'gouti was growling and throwing itself against the rusted BRC wire.

Don't be vex, he said. He knows me, like I told you.

Me and you will work something out, he said and touched his nose to mine, then turned and followed the sound of the cows.

❧

I followed the well-trodden path back to Bacolet Trace and into Scarborough proper. Then, through the streets of the town and up Fort Street to the General Hospital on Fort King George that overlooked the crisscrossed streets, the close-together houses, the clustered harbor, and the blue water then the dark blue that marked the beginning of the Caribbean Sea.

The morning went by quickly. I collected the sheets and towels from the canvas bin on the ward and took them to the wash house near the bell tank, a round metal building, like an overturned bowl, with an iron gate at the front. Teresa and Sherva were already there, standing at the washtubs, rubbing clothes along the scrubbing board that looked like a row of steep concrete stairs along the inside of the tub. From the door, it looked like they were washing clouds, white clothes among thick, white suds. I went next to Sherva, said a quick good morning, plugged my tub with the rubber stopper, and grabbed the bucket to fill it at the brass standpipe.

Eh eh, yuh nuh see am? Teresa said to my back. She reach late an' ah talk 'bout good marning. Ah good day dis!

Teresa was as ugly as she sounded. Short and squat.

Hands broad and veiny from washing everybody's clothes in the whole of Plymouth to feed her short, squat children.

Leave she dis marning. Yuh nuh see she face fulla trouble. Sherva had finished the first of her morning batch and had thrown another in the soap water.

I am fine. Just feeling a little sick. I poured water in my tub.

Sick? Yuh ah breed, town ghul? Teresa again.

This wouldn't bother me any other day. But today Teresa's taunt was true. She had five children and I wondered if she was one of those village women who could tell a woman was pregnant from the smell of her perspiration or from the way she walked. I fixed my face with a smile. I'm sick of you, Teresa. You know that? Sick of your backward, Bottom-side talk and your face that is as broad and as black as a coal pot, so early in the morning.

See. Is you wha' start she up, Sherva said and started washing. The soap made a squeaky rhythm as she washed cotton sheets and diapers from the maternity ward with both hands, and only used the tub's concrete scrubber to rub out stains.

Teresa sucked her teeth and was silent.

I sorted my first batch and threw them into the tub with some disinfectant. I left clothes with heavy stains, blood and toto, black stains that I don't think could come from a human, to soak at the bottom of the tub to wash later, and soaped up the rest with my hard blue soap.

The washing, and the nice breeze blowing at this height across the Fort, made me forget about Leo's face looking toward the cows and not at me. At tea break, I went to use the lavatory and realized I had left my drawers in the bush house. I was so taken up with telling him and Leo not saying the things I thought he was going to say that I forgot it. I pictured the white cotton thing on the small table where Leo and me—I mean Leo and I—had tea from a burnt cup when we were hungry after breaking our one- or two-day fast from each other.

I wasn't sure if to be vexed with myself or with Leo or Teresa for clucking her tongue and laughing at nothing. I wanted to go back to the bush house right then. The door wasn't locked, just kept closed with a piece of wood that spins on a nail to keep the door from swinging open. Anybody could go there and find my bloomers. And take it to the obeah man and do something to me. Even Ann might find it and kill my child or mash up Leo and I.

I ate my biscuits and tea quickly and went back to the tubs. I didn't take the whole lunch, and slapdashed the bedding that wasn't soiled, washed soiled spots on the ones I was soaking, rinsed everything fast, fast and was waiting to sign out by half past two.

In Bacolet, the river mumbled secrets the mountain told it on the way down. I wondered what the river said about me, because, sometimes, when Leo and I had the wild feeling that people like us get, he lifted me up and we straddled, standing up, open air, my body thrown back, my fingers touching the ground. The thought now made a wetness between my legs. Too bad nobody but the crayfish and the short grass near the water understood what the water was talking about. Overhead, birds made crisp chirps in the trees. I spun the wooden latch, went in, and put on my drawers in the mostly dark. Bright light sliced the walls in places.

Back in town, as I walked up the dirt hill to the house where I lived with my mother, I passed through a cloud of sweet with spice at the end of the scent. Coconut sweetbread. As I neared the house, I saw Mammy at the dirt oven, near the guinep tree, with something on the wooden peel.

Ohhh, Betty coming, I called out to her so she will know that it wasn't the voice of some spirit on the wind.

Aiiiiii, she answered without looking back, and carried the peel with two sweetbreads to the kitchen at the left of the house.

I passed her and went to the base of the four steps at the side of the house that led to the drawing room. Tired. No strength to go up. Mammy put two more pans of sweetbread in the kitchen, hung the peel on the nail and came to me. Before I thought about what I was going to say, I was crying.

Let us retire inside, Mammy said, held my hand and helped me up the steps.

In the drawing room, I sat on the settee and drank

the water she gave me. Then she brought me sweet-bread. A broken-off end with caramelized sugar and slightly burnt raisins. Sweetbread makes me feel better. Black fruitcake makes me feel best.

Mammy didn't ask what happened. She told me to bathe and change and went to wash the nice glass she had taken from the wagonette so I could drink the water. I was glad to be told what to do, because I couldn't think for myself. I only thought of the dundun drum–sized space that was going to be left if Leo and me—and I—were to… I can't even say it.

Later, after dinner, we sat in the drawing room. One kerosene lamp, the smoldering orange end of a mosquito coil, and the glow of Mammy's pipe jumbled the shadows and made Mammy's face look like the bricks on the powder house at the fort. I told her all that had happened that day.

Hmmm. What exactly you want?

I want Leonard, Mammy.

That is all? You want a man?

I want Leonard. Not a man. Leonard.

What in the way of what you want?

Ann. People's mouths when they find out.

That's all. Mammy drew on the pipe and blew out the smoke, a ghost among the

overlapping shadows.

Ann is—this dark room full of smoke and shadows was the only place I could say this out loud—Ann is Leo's common-law wife. And my niece, Mammy.

Ahhh, we at the root of it. She sucked the pipe, tapped the mosquito coil, and ash fell off in a soft gray curve.

I think he wants to leave me, Mammy. Make me look like a fool in front of the whole of Tobago, from Crown Point to Charlotteville.

You sure? I don't read him like that.

I don't understand how.

How what?

How he could want her more than me. Me and he is—

Him and I are—, Mammy started.

Him and I are the same. And she is so…so black. I am more beautiful than Ann. He said so. I am the most beautiful woman in all of Tobago. Leo is the best-looking man anybody ever saw. Him and I are a match.

What you want? She held the pipe at the corner of her mouth.

I could hold him and make him never leave me. Make him leave Ann. Take his hair to Brothers in Plymouth and make him stay with me and forget about she as long as he live.

Her. Forget about her.

Yes, her.

Leonard is a butcher in Town Market, who makes a good sale every Saturday, Mammy drew on her pipe and continued. He leaves his cows to pasture in Bacolet and nobody steals them. Ann has a shop by her house, and a stall near Manny Rum Shop. You think these people stupid? You might get through at first, but when they go to check their business and find out it's you who in their way, dey go tu'n yuh ovah! An' you an' yuh pickney go dead an' bury. Is that what you want?

No, Mammy. But what to do?

Go see him tomorrow as normal. All men get surprised when they hear 'bout a baby.

I waited.

And stop keeping this secret.

How?

Let people know you and him are together.

But Ann?

You past that. Past that since the first day he asked you to come see him in Bacolet and you went. People knowing will help you. If anything happens to you, villagegram will say that Ann do it. She's an Anglican, big in the church, and needs to look good. And she knows my hands not pocked, because if she go out for you, mi ah go ah Charlotteville fuh she an' she pickney-dem. Mammy released the ash from the coil.

You will get a Charlotteville wokman for me, Mammy?

I will pass Plymouth and go straight to the end of the island to find the best obeah man. I promise you that! She slapped her thigh.

We laughed, noising up the night.

I tell you I will walk to Charlotteville, right? She laughed, spilling a little smoldering tobacco from her pipe onto her lap. Then she flicked the false candle fly onto the floor.

I got up and covered the embers with the base of my enamel cup, ending the danger to our two-room wooden house on concrete piles.

My body was like air and I touched my belly, hopeful for the future, like I was when I washed myself at the river earlier that day. Mammy smoked the last of her pipe, rinsed her mouth at the back window, and went to bed.

I sat for an hour or so more, listening to cricket songs, the galvanized roof's crackling as it contracted in the cool night. Then, as I turned down the lamp and moved the coil to the bedroom, I replayed our conversation and chuckled to myself. Thoughts of what I was going to say to Leo the next day and how I was going to let Tobago people know my business and still smell like a rose were trying to surface. But I wrapped them up in the *Royal Gazette* and pushed them down to a place I had for those things, like a broken teacup that you wrapped up so it wouldn't hurt anybody. The teacup was pushed so far down that I slept a deep dreamless sleep, weary from the long day.

❧

The next morning, in Bacolet, Leo was wild. When I approached the bush house, he pushed open the door and said, I could smell yuh, enno.

There was no wildness in me that day. But all of me

was bruised from the day before, a bruise that only the touch of flesh could salve. So I obliged the ocelot he was that morning. I stripped to my petticoat and gave the river something to tell the sea when they met in the muddy delta later that day.

When we were done, we lay on our clothes on a worn dirt patch behind the bush house, looking up at a clear blue sky. A sign that we will find clarity in this situation?

Cows, who had eaten the grass within the circle that their rope allowed, moaned deeply for Leo in the distance.

I sat up and looked down at him, and at the light-brown cotton shirt near his head to see if a strand of hair was caught in the fabric. I could take it, easy, easy, when he went to pee. I ought to have insurance if I was going to take a risk and make a child.

Have the baby, he said without looking at me. He turned and studied my face, like he was seeing me for the first time. Ann will never understand. You hear?

I looked up at the sky and smiled. Clarity.

He put his head on my lap, then got on his elbows and cupped my belly in both hands. We bind together now, he said, then got up and peed in the bushes at the edges of the clearing, his long back to me. After we dressed, he gathered his tools to answer the morning call and I went to the river to rinse the wildness from between my legs and put on my drawers. All of me was covered and complete.

❧

A few days later, early on Friday morning, Mammy and I were brushing our teeth with ashes at the back of the house, when we heard Leo saying good morning from the front yard.

Mammy rinsed her mouth and went to meet him.

It was not fully daylight; only the sun's forehead was visible. People in the houses on the hill were starting to stir. Lamplight shimmered behind curtains.

When I got to the front, Leo was under the guinep tree, akimbo with a crocus bag at his feet. He brought provisions. Green bananas, cassava, and bush mangoes.

Mammy pointed at the bag with her chin. She held up a parcel wrapped in brown paper. And beef, she said.

Beef bones too, Leo said. To make soup. Strengthen you and the child.

Thank you, I said. I was worried that the neighbors, cousins, and semi-cousins, all living on family land, might see him. Then remembered I ought to let people know. The hill was a good place to start. But it was abattoir day, and Leo couldn't stay.

Well, he said. Betty. Miss Ailith. Later. He went down the hill and onto Cane Street.

Every week after that, he brought a new crocus bag of provisions and took away the empty one. We continued to meet in Bacolet, on the same days, Monday, Wednesday, and Thursday.

When I started to get big, by five months, we found

other ways to join together. But it was different, as there was a tide inside me that remained high and had no low. I craved him more than before. Sometimes he was afraid and stopped in the middle of our business to ask if I was alright. Those times, he looked as innocent as a rabbit, eyes darting, voice like new leaves in the wind. When I nodded yes and touched his hips so he could continue, he moved as if I was made of glass and he would break me. Afterwards, he said, you too much for a woman sometimes, Betty. Too much.

❦

Teresa, with her inquisitive self, noticed me sitting and washing with my legs closed at one side of the tub. When she asked me what was the matter, I told her straight that I was pregnant for Leonard.

The music of her rubbing bedding against the washing board stopped. Leonard Alfred from right in town dey? she asked.

I pretended not to hear her and washed a baby's chemise that had two small dark-brown stains, blood maybe. I put the stains between my fingers and rubbed the brown circles until they were gone.

He han'some suh tay, Teresa continued. An' him have plenty prapaty all over 'bago. Yuh do good, ghul.

I felt Sherva watching me and turned so our eyes made four.

Dat is not Ann Leonard, over on Broad Street? She husban'? Right down de road dey?

Ann don't have a husband, I said.

Hmm, Sherva said, and went back to her washing, a wall between her and I after that.

He mus' be hang good an' nice too. Teresa pierced the silence Sherva made and held her crotch, roughly. He ah go inside yuh pum pum, smooth an' straight, like bucket inna well. Yuh ah lucky ghul. Mi nevah had nothin' like ah dat suh.

After that day, something in Teresa recognized something in me, and we didn't argue anymore.

୭

Leo gave me two pounds a week so I could prepare. I had a crib made out of teak from Trinidad. When the man, an ace carpenter from Speyside, came to drop it off, I talked to his wife, who painted and varnished the goods they made, and told her who the father was. She didn't know Leo, but telling them, business people who had customers here and there, meant that people in Speyside might know.

Mammy brought me a Singer and I made white cotton diapers and chemises in blues and pinks and yellows.

୭

I was seven months when Ann came. I had come home from work and was in the kitchen kneading flour to fry bakes in tallow later that evening. Mammy's uncle in Whim had died, and she went to help with the cooking for the wake and to prepare for the funeral. I couldn't go because pregnant women couldn't be near the dead or go in the graveyard. I covered the dough so it would rise a little and came out of the kitchen to find Ann in the yard, under the guinep tree, where Leonard had stood when he brought a hog leg three days before. She was in a plain, loose maternity frock and a head tie. Belly big and carrying low. Tall like Leo, her back straight. The tree cast a shadow on her face.

I come to see for myself, she said.

I closed the bottom half of the kitchen door, went near the house, and eyed her, her body tense like a mapepire about to spring.

She came toward me, and I expected her to box me in my face or push me down. But she turned and went to the kitchen. Hanging on a nail at the top part of the kitchen door was an empty crocus bag that Leonard had brought, filled with provisions, days before. Mammy had packed the yams and a hand of plantain in a parcel, put it on her head, and carried it as her contribution to the wake.

Ann put one hand behind her back and held the bag with two fingers, like she was examining cloth in Kurie Store in town to make a dress. Hmmm, she made a noise in her throat, recognizing the bag that traveled between my house and hers.

She looked around the yard, at me, turned and went down the hill toward Cane.

I had been holding my breath and let it out when

her plain frock had gone from view. Then I searched the ground, dirt with short wild grass, to see if Ann had thrown anything in the yard. Powder. Beads. A strange stone that didn't look like other stones. Something to kill me and my child if I were to walk on it. Something to mash up Leonard and I. I retraced her steps and tried to avoid walking where she had walked and realized that I would have to go back to the kitchen, right where Ann was standing, to ball the dough and get the pots for the fireside. I went under the house, took the long stick with the nail attached for picking guinep, and used it to shake the lower half of the door until the cabin hook slipped out and the door swung open. I used the stick to knock the crocus bag off the top part of the door. It fell on the ground like a ragged dress. I went to the side of the open kitchen door, careful to avoid where Ann had walked, and went in. My heart beat in my temples as I uncovered the enamel basin of water and poured salt in it. I filled my hand with the brine and sprinkled the saltwater at the door, in front of the kitchen, then stepped into the yard. I sprinkled as I retraced Ann's steps until there was saltwater in the entire front yard and on the crocus bag. Down the hill where she went. Mr. Walton, who lived behind us, was coming up the hill, two pieces of lumber on one shoulder. When he saw me, he came off the path, turned and told his wife, who I hadn't noticed, Nuh walk deh. The wife, a thin woman with legs like a yard fowl, looked through me, moved her cloth-wrapped parcel from her head to her hands and followed her husband as he made his own way in the low shrubs that lined the dirt path. I sprinkled to Cane Street and threw the last of the water in the direction that Ann went. Good riddance, I whispered, and flung my hands in the direction of my lover's common-law wife, to chase her and thoughts of her away.

⤕

On Wednesday, in Bacolet, the bush house was empty. Leo's stick and cutlass were gone. He had come early and left. My footfalls on the wooden floor echoed against the galvanized roof of the five-by-seven structure. The empty house, with only the sounds I made talking back to me, was a taste of what it might be like if Leo left me. Outside, there were cow sounds on the wind. He was probably almost to the other side of Bacolet by now. The soil was dark and damp from bush rain that fell, sudden and warm, and left the air cool and full of water. I am a stupid woman to be in a clearing in the bush with my big belly and can't follow Leo through the pasture land. A vexation came and I had the urge to call his name so that the wind would carry the sound and box his ears. The pregnant river taunted me.

I went to work, and had to say something nasty to shut Teresa up from talking about Leonard. Yes, she looked up to me now. But I hadn't seen or heard from Leo since Ann's visit and I wasn't sure what to think, so couldn't bear to hear Leo's name when it could be that he was finished with me and this belly. Sherva washed in silence, the wall still up.

Leonard wasn't there the Thursday either. Mammy wasn't back yet, so I couldn't ask her what to do. I couldn't sleep. Every shadow in the house danced around me.

∽

On Saturday, I went to the market in town to find him. It was just after five o'clock, from the bell at the Anglican church that Ann and her children went to. The sky was school-uniform navy, and the light of a few kerosene lamps made the market into a fairy place that might disappear when the sun had fully woken up. Vendors were still setting up their stalls. Men and women carried goods in wheelbarrows and on donkey carts. There were a few cars, the trunks laden with provisions and fruits for sale.

My nose caught a scent, like metal rust and sugar. Blood in the meat market. I followed the rusty sweetness until I saw two men in white flour-bag aprons talking near a rickety wooden table on one side of a wide paved concrete aisle. At the other side of the aisle, in the back of a stall, a man was bent over in the fairy light. There was something familiar about the shape of his elbow and the deliberate way his arm moved as he did whatever he was doing just out of view. The baby kicked as the man stood up to put a wooden cutting board on the table. Leo.

What you doing here? His eyes widened like he was surprised to see me.

You don't graze in Bacolet no more? I stepped closer to the stall. All around me, other butchers traveled down the aisle to set up. There were men alone, who parked donkey carts near the entrance and carted bags of meat from animals killed the day before. The carcasses were hung in the abattoir overnight to drain the blood so the meat wouldn't spoil fast. Some men brought their wives and others their sons to cart meat and, once Tobago people filled the market, cut pieces to order. Whatever didn't sell, butchers took home for their own families.

This is no place for you, Leo said. I will meet you up the hill when market close.

I lifted the hem of my cotton skirt and moved behind the stall, but couldn't go farther as there was a large wooden bin filled with meat.

Careful, he said, and moved from behind the bin toward me.

Freddy, yuh deh good, man? a voice asked.

I turned to face the voice so whoever said it could see my belly. Mammy was a wise woman. It was one of the two men who were talking near the entrance.

Mi deh good, Solow. Leo kept his eyes on my face.

Jus' tell ah we if yuh need any help, the shorter of the two said. Any help at all. The man grinned and showed his large jackass teeth.

I held Leo's arm at the elbow. My Leo was a man above these men.

Marning, pretty Miss. The taller one bent his head and touched the front of his straw hat as he went. I followed the red band on the hat, as he walked among the people coming and going. He looked back at me, but I turned toward Leo so didn't see when he turned away.

Come, Leo said.

I followed him out the meat market, along a path where the lamplight didn't reach. When we were in a dark patch, a basin of silence among the noise, he leaned his face close to mine.

One of Ann family saw us walking out Bacolet together, he said.

She came to drop obeah in my yard on Monday.

Eh suh? He froze.

Of course, eh suh, I shouted so he would know I was angry.

She wouldn't do you anything. That child is mine and she wouldn't do that to me.

You still grazing in Bacolet? I had to know.

Betty. I told you Ann wouldn't understand. You and she is close family. So I have to be on Broad Street these days.

The sun peeped over the horizon to see what people were doing, lightening the navy blue. Our patch of dark wouldn't last much longer.

I waited.

When things cool, I will send for you. But you getting big now. He pointed at my belly.

The light moved in to rinse the darkness like stains on clothes.

Seven months, I said and touched my belly. I didn't look but felt eyes on me. Us. And the noises got quiet near us, like we were doing something important and people hushed themselves out of respect.

I know, he said.

It's still there, you know, just taking shelter, I said and slid my hand down my belly to my crotch.

That is why, he paused, that is why... That is why. He smiled and shook his head. Don't worry, I will take some shelter in Bacolet just now. He touched his forehead to mine, turned and made long strides to his stall, where customers had already gathered.

༄

He sent for me two weeks later. One afternoon, somebody's child came up the hill and bawled marniiiing until Mammy and I went in the gallery.

Mi lookin' fuh Miss Beatrice. He was naked except for khaki schoolboy pants with holes all over it.

Don't shout the message from the front yard, Mammy said. Come inside to tell us.

The boy walked to the space in the wooden gallery railing and came in, his ten toes on the wood floor. Mr. Alfred sey Miss Beatrice cyan tek shelter from tomarrow.

Mammy looked at me, a question in her face.

Something we talk, the other day, I said and smiled.

Okay, Mammy said.

The boy waited and twisted his body to scratch his back with one hand and a red circular sore on his shin. He wiped whatever came off the sore on his pants.

He paid you? I asked.

A shilling. But de Mister sey yuh go gimme a Redspot.

Alright, I said, and got up. My legs were swollen from washing earlier that day, straight and stiff like legs on a new-stuffed doll.

You stay, Mammy said, and went to get the sweet drink.

The boy smiled, and showed straight white teeth that didn't belong in his dirty face.

Going back to Bacolet didn't mean that Ann had an understanding. It meant that Leo and I had one. An understanding. And that was all that mattered. There was another reason, too, that we had to keep having relations. It helped the baby to come easier, to slip out of me when the time came. I could drink boiled ochres for that, but that was for women who went with a man they met in a village harvest and never saw him again. Never told him he had a child. That wasn't me. I had a man and my child had a father.

✍

I ordered two crochet hats, two booties, and seven bodices from Molly, a woman from Roxborough, who makes them nice, like they came from England. I got blankets and everything to prepare. Mammy made me a blue cotton sack to pin on the baby, to stop the evil eye.

By eight and a half months, I was full like a breadfruit, skin tight, legs too swollen to put on my shoes. I stopped the washing. Bacolet was too much. The child slept on the spot where my torso met my right leg, so that leg was numb, heavy.

One morning, I came out of the bathroom and was walking up the steps when my water came down, wetting the steps and the house dress I had on.

I bawled for Mammy, who was in the kitchen.

Ohhh, she answered me.

Come quick, I shouted.

I here. Mammy had a look on her face.

What happen?

Go on up the steps. You in any pain? Her eyes left my face and went to my legs. I followed her gaze and saw red streaks in the water that had fallen on the steps.

That happens sometimes, Mammy said. Go inside. One of Astrid's boys will get Mr. Gray. She held my hand and guided me up the steps to the bedroom.

By the time Mr. Gray's car pulled up Fort Street to the hospital door, pain bloomed like ink spreading in water in my lower back. I held on to Mammy's hand in the back seat.

What the blood mean? I whispered to her for the third time.

The doctor will tell us. She got out and went around

to my side of the car, held my hands as I rocked my way forward and out of the Renault.

Mr. Gray walked ahead of us with the bag of clothes and baby things. I've been washing at Scarborough General for two years and had never walked in the front door. Just came up the hill, took the dirty clothes from the wards, and went straight to the wash house. As I waddled in, a nurse in a pink uniform and a hat like a paper boat called for the orderly, a thin man in a white gabardine jacket that was too big for him, to bring a wooden wheelchair. I sat down and let the people around me take over, the pain in my back more than me. I. Me.

The labor lasted eight chimings of the bell at the Anglican church. I bled more during the labor so, by the time my daughter was born, the room was filled with black and brown doctors and nurses, with sweat on their brows and eyes that only looked at me when my child screamed to say that she had arrived in the land of the living.

The matron, Ann's cousin, put the baby on my chest, as if she was resting down a fork after she ate. She talked to the doctors as if I wasn't there, cut the cord, and asked the nurse to tidy me up.

Fiona was beautiful. Fair with reddish hair, the same texture as Leo's soil. Her face more like mine and Mammy's. She didn't take much more for Leo.

When I nursed her for the first time, Mammy pinned the blue sack to the chemise near the baby's chest. How you feel? Any pain? Mammy wanted to know.

A little when she's nursing.

I have plenty bush medicine for you when we get home.

What the blood mean, Mammy? Why you wouldn't tell me?

A part of the afterbirth came off and it bleed a little. She touched Fiona's head. She look like a queen. Ent? My granddaughter, my Queenie.

Mammy? I moved the baby away from her.

It might mean that blood might spill in the yard. Her fingers traced the swirls of hair that framed Fiona's face.

I regretted that I didn't let the question stay in the yard, lingering on the steps like a neighbor waiting to be let in the door. I always had to press things. I pressed Leo. I pressed Teresa. Now I pressed Mammy and wished I never heard those words about the yard. And blood. And my daughter, who I already know I am going to love the most of all the other children I will have. Because she is something Leo and I made together. I will not press her like I do other people.

God Almighty, help me to be a better person.

You alright? Mammy interrupted my thoughts.

What was that you call her?

What, Queenie?

Yeah. That is a nice nickname for her. Right, Queenie? You like that? I put my nose at her neck and inhaled her sweet, creamy love smell.

Her eyes were still closed, reddish-blonde lashes on

her cheeks, and her warm breath against my breast. It would be twenty-one days before she opened her eyes. I hoped she would open them when I was nursing her, so the first person she saw in the world would be me.

Show me you can hold back furious tides
from the sea of yourself,
beach desire to make entire cities comfortable.

– FROM THE POEM "DARK,"
A. K. HERMAN, 2023

Love Story No. 8:
Jane and Phillip

TO SEDUCE HIS neighbor's wife, Mrs. Alice Brown, Mr. Cromwell hired a landscaper to create an English garden around his Port-of-Spain mansion. His own wife, Mrs. Cromwell, had succumbed to Wide Sargasso Sea madness and returned to London just after their daughter Jane was born. So, Cromwell, with his curly hair and tanned looks, was marooned in British Trinidad with a teenage daughter.

The garden was to be a sprawling thing of red and yellow roses, hibiscuses, crotons, tropical palms, and a fake ruined bridge. So, the landscaper (occasional rag-picker and prostitute when money got tight) was there every day in shorts and bare chest working the cutlass and shovel with veined hands covered in dirt.

One afternoon, the landscaper sighed, brushed

sweat from his brow and looked up to see Jane undressing at her bedroom window. He stopped his work and a caged, zealous thing leapt from his eyes to Jane's, reddening her cheek. She touched her hot face and closed the curtains.

For two weeks, Jane held the landscaper's gaze and undressed to her petticoat before the open window. One day, a strap of the petticoat slipped from her shoulders and the landscaper dropped his tools and strode through the servants' entrance to Jane's bedroom, where such ripe fruit was easily splayed and eaten, the communion marked by dirt and crushed leaves on the white cotton sheets with eyelet trim.

In the meantime, Cromwell read poetry to Alice Brown on her narrow settee, while she commented on his evolving garden. Theirs, a proper seduction by the book!

∽

They did it twice more in Jane's bedroom.

Five times in the tool shed behind the mansion.

The roses flowered at about the same time Jane did. And the landscaper took her to a place where girls went to have their insides caressed with a hatpin to terminate their mistakes. When it was over, he kissed her cold cheek and took her home.

The next morning, the maid found Jane, pale and feverish in a blood-soaked bed. Soon, island doctors filled the frilly bedroom and, after they took Cromwell's money, declared that the innocent girl was raped and left for dead.

To find the rapist, Cromwell plotted with his neighbor Mr. Brown and spent his money in Port-of-Spain's low places until a name surfaced: Phillip B. Douglas, Landscaper (occasional rag-picker and prostitute when money got tight).

It was Brown who picked Phillip from among the streetwalkers on Charlotte Street, took him home, kissed him and drugged him. With regret, Brown then took Phillip to the tool shed where Cromwell beat the young man with the side of a cutlass, slit his throat and planted his ruined corpse under a row of palm trees.

For one year, Jane waited at her bedroom window for Phillip's return. When he did not show, she shuttered her heart and went to London where the cold drizzle and fog suited her. After saying goodbye to Jane at the Port-of-Spain wharf, Cromwell went straight to Mr. Brown's house and sat with Alice on her narrow settee. Touching her thigh, he asked her to choose any flower that he might grow it in his garden. Alice blushed. You must grow more trees, she whispered, handsome palms with branches like arms and legs flapping wildly about. Cromwell was a bit startled, but collected himself and kissed Alice mightily until she forgot the matter.

"I know you is the one for my Sunil, but he hand in the lion mouth with that girl and she family."

— Mrs. Suinarine, 2012

Inside

AFTERWARDS, I STAYED in the position that Sunil had left me before he went to the bathroom. I was trying to read my body like it was a handful of bones thrown on the sheet. It was missionary that time, legs spread, arms on either side of my head with the elbows bent, palms open. Sunil had put my panty, a white lacy thing, across my stomach so it wouldn't make that sound he hated. My belly has two folds of fat, one just under my bobbies, and another under my navel. The flat place between the fat sweats when we're doing it, and it makes this noise, like trying to pull your foot out of thick mud. A song came from between my legs. Hmmm. If anything was slightly off it was the bobbies. I touched one and looked at the brown swelling with its large nipple like a raisin hat. Sunil barely touched them throughout the whole business. Weird. Last year, on his last night in Trinidad, I had to beg him to stop trying to suck my heart through them. He looked up at me, laughed then his pale cheeks turned red and, before I knew it, he was crying and talking with webs of saliva across the cave of his mouth. "I don't want to go, Resh. Tell your father to cash the ticket and I could stay. Me and you…blah, blah, blah…could get married…have a good life in Trinidad…" He had no land, no business, nothing, and wanted to get married to a woman like me. Daddy was sending him to school and planned to give him some businesses to run when he returned to Trini. That way poor Sunil from Princes Town would have more than looks when we get married.

The water stopped falling in the shower and I looked up at the ceiling and at the walls. A single, uncovered light bulb was at the center of a stucco ceiling above the bed. Glossy white paint showed every pit and dried paint drip on the walls. Effing ugly.

"What you thinking about?" His voice was the same. Deep. I felt it in my chest. He held the towel around his waist with one hand. I closed my legs and turned to face him. The roses he had given me at the airport the night before were in a vase on the nightstand. They smelled sour and the edges of the petals were black.

"About the fock."

"What?" He laughed and the gray eyes that caught my attention in secondary school ten years ago sparkled, like a cream soda in a glass in the sun. He got handsomer since he went away.

"You hiding from me, Sunil?" I pointed at the towel. "I done see everything so—"

"Resh, you start to give trouble already?" He smiled, retied the towel around his chest, held the knot with one hand, and pursed his lips.

I sat up. "Let the towel go."

He sucked his teeth, the sound like a bicycle gear coming to a stop.

"I want to see the thing Daddy send away."

He let the towel go.

"Turn around."

He turned his ass to me.

"No, not so." I laughed. "I want to see it from the side, to see if it hanging right."

"Resh, you ain't change, oui. Still crazy." He turned and put both palms behind his head. I watched every crease. Every hair. I was wondering how he thought the sex was. But if I asked him, he might know that I cared about what he thought. Not my scene to come off like that.

"You finish?" He gyrated his hips then thrust them forward, everything swinging.

"Sunil, stop! I still looking… Okay, okay, I done. The hair too long. Trim it like you used to have it."

He nodded and walked around the bed to the chest of drawers to get dressed.

"You going to trim it, right?"

"Resh, I leaving my balls just so. I can't even tell you how to cut your hair." He zipped his pants up. "You not getting up to bathe?"

I was kinda annoyed about the balls comment, but

couldn't stop looking at the walls. It was like each dent was pulling me in.

"You don't like the place?" he asked.

"No, is not…I know you don't like to talk about money, Sunil, but if you needed more money to live on, you could've told me, and I or Daddy could've—"

"Resh, you and your father paying for school, giving me a allowance every month. I comfortable here."

"Is just that I thought…I thought it would've been nicer. We talk on the phone all the time and you never say it was like this. The area nice? At least?"

"This is Brooklyn. East Flatbush. Is a nice area." A line formed on his forehead. "But it always have something nicer. And this place might look bad compared to…what you accustomed to, but the rent here is high, even for Brooklyn. Plus, the woman who own the house, Mrs. Mannix, she from Antigua, she don't bother me. You should hear the horror stories other people who come to this country have. Coming home and finding the landlord in your place, people making noise so you can't study…"

While he talked, he folded his arms and, with one hand, played with his chest hairs. I looked at the fingers pulling the thick dark hairs then back to his mouth, like Shahid Kapoor's mouth.

"…not fixing anything. And Caribbean people are the worst landlords. They just don't get the tenant thing. They think anybody living in their house is a child even if they paying rent." He stopped, took a T-shirt from the drawer, and put it on. "You don't know, Resh. You don't know."

"I forget how you could go on and on when you want to make a point. I get it. You comfortable here and you don't want we money." I was effing vex. The idea that he would bring me to a place like this then try to justify it by making it about money. Like he ever had to think about money since we been together. I wrapped the sheet around me and got up.

"Now you hiding from me," Sunil said.

I didn't answer.

"You vex, Resh? Don't be vex. You just reach. You want to stay in the hotel instead? I could stay there with you till you leave."

"No, I go stay." I went to the bathroom.

✎

The next day, a Thursday, after Sunil went to class, I tried to watch TV on my laptop, but Daddy and my sister, Sharma, kept texting me. Sharma and me manage two stores and a nightclub, Club Space. Every text was about deliveries, workers and the band for Saturday. I texted Daddy to say that I was alright and told Sharma to do whatever. I was on vacation, for eff sake.

In the bedroom, Sunil had made the bed. The roses were bent over, trying to kiss the nightstand with their stale, red lips. I lifted the mattress. An old T-shirt and a pair of jeans lay on top of four wide planks of plywood that ran across a metal frame. There were clothes in all the drawers. Not a lot. I checked the tags. Regular brands. And two pairs of shoes under the bed, some brown leather dressy business and sneakers. That's three pairs, counting the one he was wearing. A few things in the closet. No coats. I showered, got dressed and went out.

Outside was so bright that I had to cover my eyes from the white light bouncing off the chrome of cars parked across the street. I walked up the narrow, bare concrete steps that led from Sunil's basement apartment to the yard. Spring was teasing the yard and a few light-blue flowers littered the short grass. I went up some red-painted steps to the front door of the house. I didn't notice the night before, but it was a gray brownstone. The door was varnished wood with clear glass panels. Just inside the door, I saw some flip-flops and a woman's worn, black strappy sandals. I pressed the white doorbell that jutted from the wall like a pimple. Nothing. Again. Footsteps came toward the door.

Mrs. Mannix opened the inner door, varnished wood too, and looked out. She narrowed her eyes and leaned her head to one side so I waved and pointed toward the basement. She mouthed, Oh, and opened the door.

"Hello, I'm Sunil girlfriend. Reshma Boodoo." I shook her hand.

"Yes. He tell me you was comin', see." Her gray hair was in plaits like a girl.

"I just wanted to say hello. In case you see me in the yard and was wondering who I was."

"Okay. You had a good flight comin' in?"

"Yes. Smooth. I landed, right?" I laughed because I didn't know what else to do. "So, Sunil ask me to pay the rent. He didn't have any time this morning." I took out the money. "How much, again?"

"Rent not due till next week. He payin' early?" I saw her round shoulders move back under the shiny, yellow polyester.

"Yes. We mightn't be here next week. How much? He forget to separate the rent money from the bills money."

"Seven."

I counted it out.

"Wait for a receipt." She turned and went inside.

As I walked along Troy Avenue and turned onto Church Avenue, I heard the receipt crinkling in the pocket of my leather jacket and shoved it in deeper. It was just before midday, so there were few people on the street. I had been to New York many times, but never to a poor-people place like this. I passed stores with racks of clothes outside that said *3 for $20*. There seemed to be a vegetable market on every corner with rows of oranges, pears, apples, and other goods inside and outside. I watched a man cut the blackened, spongy ends from some carrots with a short cutlass, wrap them in plastic and Styrofoam and put them on a table with other fruits and vegetables and a sign that said *50c Any* *one.* In between the cheap clothes, vege-marts, and beauty stores were churches. Church of Christ. Eglise Baptiste Haitienne. They opened right on the pavement, some of them next to restaurants with only a gate to, I suppose, separate the sheep from the goats. The fanciest shoulder-high gate was in front one New Community Church. A short fella in a shining technicolor outfit, like country come to town, was behind it. He told me good morning and asked me if God was good. And all I could think of was the receipt in my pocket and how I was searching Sunil's place. I held my head up and walked to the train station at Nostrand Avenue. The little technicolor man started singing some hymn. The sound stayed in my head long after I could actually hear him. Even the rumbling of the subway train couldn't drown it out.

Later that day, I heard Sunil fumbling with the keys and got up from the couch to meet him at the door then sat down and pretended to stare at the laptop. I let him call me twice before I answered. "Yeah." You must never be eager.

"Hon, you stay inside whole day?" He was at the living room door. When I didn't turn around, he walked over and kissed me on the cheek. He smelled like cologne plus clothes plus a slight sweaty, man smell. The lower fold of my belly pitched forward a little. Okay, a lot.

"You went out?" He put down his knapsack.

I turned around and shrugged. "No, I wear makeup to stay home."

He smiled. "You eat something? Want me to buy some food?"

"Yeah. I kinda hungry. But…"

"But?"

"I got some things for you today."

"Oh Lord, Resh." He said it like he was fed-up or something.

My face was probably looking vexed, because he changed his tune. "What you get?"

I ran past him to the bedroom and pointed to the bags on the floor.

"Saks?" He sighed loudly.

"I see you don't have any good clothes. And you need sheets for this bed. Plus, I want to go out. Party."

He sat on the bed and I reached for the first bag. "I want to go this Saturday. And I want to see your school, Brock College."

"Baruch College. Bah-rook." He lifted his small, womanish chin.

"Look at you nah? Telling me how to pronounce. Fine, I want to see Baruch College and, when we finish trying on clothes, I want something to eat. Nothing from around here." I wrinkled my face. "Call a restaurant from somewhere else."

He seemed frozen, looking at me and at the same time looking past me to the bathroom door.

"Sunil, you hear me?"

"Yes. Try on. Food. Party Saturday. Show she Bah-rook."

"Okay. Try this one on first." I picked up a bag and took out a blazer.

He was staring past me again.

"Sunil?"

"Reshma?" he mocked.

⌁

On Saturday, my father called. He wanted to make sure I wasn't staying with Sunil. In this day and age, Daddy trying to convince himself that Sharma and me are pure. Geez.

"No, Daddy. I at the hotel and Sunil coming to pick me up." I put one finger across my lips when Sunil came out the bathroom and pointed at the phone. Then Daddy was going on about the store in San Fernando and blah, blah, blah. Then his voice got schoolteacherish. "Reshma, how things going with Sunil?"

"How you mean?" I changed the tone of my voice to match his.

"He alright? He going to school?"

I walked to the farthest corner of the living room. "He in school. Going to see the school next week."

"Okay, that is all I want to know. Because people tell me not to do this thing. Not to send a next man son to school and give him business to run. The pundit and all say is not a good thing. That I lucky with girl children and not boy children. And is not…"

Sunil came into the room and spun around. He was

155

in the Zegna pale pinkish, taupish, don't know how to describe it, cotton pants, with the navy Zegna blazer and white shirt. Some pale Calvin sneakers to bring it down a notch.

Daddy was still talking. "…because you want it—"

"Daddy, Sunil reach. I have to go."

"Let me talk to him, nah?"

"Next time, we runnin' late. Call tomorrow." I touched the red bar across the screen.

I screamed. He was looking so effing hot.

"Shhh…Resh. Mrs. Mannix." He put his palms up and widened his eyes. That night they were cream soda with flecks of gold.

I went to the mirror on the closet door to check myself. The girdle panty made my stomach look flat in the red Bebe mini sheath dress. My face looked like a brown Lakshmi murti, heavy black-lined eyes and thin red lips. Black C L heels made good legs look model-great, with long, thick, dark hair to my behind. Just that alone was half of what all Indian men wanted. The other half was to know how to make sada roti from scratch. Bilnah. Ghee and Tawah. Flip it hot with one oily hand, and watch it swell like a young girl's belly, the whole nine. But my mother died when I was in primary school, so I never learned to do any of those things. Daddy never brought another woman in the house. Sharma and me grew up on KFC and buy-food. I know Daddy has a woman. Sometimes, on the phone, I hear a woman's voice in the background. Other times,

Chris, our driver, is out all day. I'm home, Daddy is home, Sharma is in the store. So who is the chauffeur chauffeuring then? When I pile in the car to go out on those evenings, the back seat smells like perfume.

That night, we went to Giocare, Aniello's club, on 50th and 9th Avenue. Aniello has a face like a Greek statue from a museum, with a short, compact, chiseled body to match. I met him when he came to my nightclub in Trinidad last year, and I had promised to visit his club when I was in New York. So we got the royal treatment. We were in the back in a private leather booth with Aniello's friends and his wife, Shari, a tall, gorgeous woman from Martinique with big wild hair and a vacant look in her brown eyes. The friends? Ehhh. Club flies I call them, because every popular club has them flitting around until they find a hotter place to go to. Oldish well-dressed businessmen-types with some pretty, pretty, thin, thin girl on their arm that they were trying to impress. There was a glass-paneled private bar with small cask whiskey, champagne, everything. Men in tight black clothes and aprons kept bringing out platters of food with shrimp and two-color caviar, and every kind of dessert you could think of. Our table had a clear crystal bowl of coke. I snorted two fingertips-worth, enough to sharpen the edges and brighten the colors. Aniello had some white pills, like coated aspirin, in his pocket. He took two after I refused him: one for me and one for him, he said.

All night, Aniello kept trying to pour Sunil's drinks. After the pills kicked in, he got brave and ran his hands along Sunil's thighs and commented on how soft the cotton on his pants was. But he had a thick Italian accent and "soft" sounded like "suck." "Tha fabreek ez sooo suck." So Sunil crossed his legs and spent most of the night away from the private booth in a chair against the wall with his face pinched, his eyes in shadow. He was too angry to notice that some of the thin, pretty girls and Shari had their doll's eyes on him too. I danced all night with Aniello, with Shari, with the club flies, with everybody. The whole time, I felt Sunil's eyes on me, gray laser beams that burned my legs and cut holes in my dress, like that fella from *X-Men*. The good-looking one with the shades, who was toting it for Jean Grey. But I never looked at Sunil once. Around three o'clock, the DJ played a soca and reggae mix for us and, just so, Sunil was up and dancing. He was behind me wining, one arm across my chest, just under my bobbies, at the top of the girdle. I bent over and gyrated on the crotch of his suck cotton pants. My hair stuck to me, like warm, wet palms holding both cheeks. Through the corner of one eye, in the mirror near the bar, I saw us. Some tall, well-dressed man was peeing a big splotch of red paint. And I laughed, loud and crazy, like an argument just under the sound of the music. I was still giggling to myself when we got in the taxi at daybreak to go home.

❧

He was kissing my stomach, and I blurted it out. "Where your coats? They not in the closet."

"Hmmm." He kissed my navel. "By the laundromat."

"And your clothes? You hardly have any clothes here. And how many coats you have?" The sensation of the last kiss lingered and I pushed it from my mind and lifted my head so I could look at him.

"Now, Resh?"

"Yeah."

He supported himself on his arms. His head and chest swung like a hammock, casting a shadow over my middle. The valley between the folds got dark. "I don't have much clothes 'cause I don't need much. My coats are in the Golden Touch Laundromat near 45th and Church Avenue." He pronounced each word like he was reading the news. "I have two coats. A dark-blue pea coat and a green down jacket. Since it is May, my leather jacket is warm enough. This is Dominic Kalipersad reporting for TV Six News."

I tried to study his face.

"Sooo, we could fock now?"

I let my head drop to the bed.

He kissed my folds and worked his way down to where the hairs began. Just when I thought he was going to come back to my lips, I felt something warm and wet between my legs. I waited to see what I would feel. Something moist, like being touched with sticky hands.

"Sunil, what you doing?"

He looked up at me and pulled his tongue in. "I thought you like that?"

"No, Sunil! I never like that."

"Resh, is—"

"I like to fock, Sunil! Dick! And throwing waist. That is me. That lickin' business is… Some girl like you to lick she, but that girl is not Reshma. Who like you to lick she?"

"How you mean?" He was supporting himself on his arms again.

"Who like you to lick she when you fock she?"

"Resh. Nobody. Is just that I wanted…to taste you. So, when you go, I could remember you. Never forget you."

His face was red and his eyes had a wet sheen to them, like he was about to cry. It was like his last night in Trinidad again and I felt like a wicked woman. I sat up, held his face in my hands and kissed him on the mouth. "Sorry, honey. Sorry. Is just that." I kissed one cheek. "You here and I there and"—I kissed the other cheek—"I hear all these stories about people going away and being with other people." I kissed his mouth again. "Sorry, sorry. Is just that the licking thing is not my scene. You know?"

He was still for a moment then he kissed my mouth and went back to my stomach. When he got to the end of that stretch of land, he worked his way up to my bobbies and neck. Once he was inside, I closed my eyes and moved fast, trying to rub away the wet sticky feeling he had put between my legs. When I was near the crest of our wave, I opened my eyes and looked up at Sunil. His eyes were like slits and there was a line in his brow, like he was trying to see something clearly. But the image wouldn't stay in my head because my mind was touching the sky.

❧

At Baruch College, we sat together at the back of a large lecture hall that slanted downwards. A tall professor in jeans lectured at the front with a red laser pointer and PowerPoint slides. Sunil introduced me to some of his friends. There was Amadou, from some country I don't remember, and the rest were people from Trinidad. There was another Sunil, fat and hairy, not like my Sunil; his girlfriend, Nadine, in a hoodie and jeans with her hair piled at the top of her head with no makeup whatsoever. And two other fellas, Jason and Brent. Brent said he was from San Fernando and that he knew me, but I didn't know him. After class, we went to a dumpling place nearby.

The dumpling place, Pot Stickers, was a long red counter with stools against a glass wall that looked out to the street, with some black chairs and small red tables at the back. We had ordered on the phone during the lecture, so we picked up and sat at one of the tables. Hairy Sunil and Nadine came with us but took their food and left. After, Sunil was telling me how Hairy

Sunil and Nadine lived together in some apartment near Baruch and wanted to open a business together. Then he started talking about how Amadou wanted to become the president of his country and that Brent and Jason were planning to return to Trinidad to get into politics.

"Anyhow." I cut him off. "How come you don't have any Indian friends?" I had my back to the door and turned around because I heard laughter and loud talking. A group of women came in, all pretty faces and dark hair.

"And Sunil and Nadine are?" He stuck a fork in a dumpling and put it in his mouth.

"I mean like *Indian* Indian. From India."

He leaned forward. "Resh, they not just from India, they from all over. Bangladesh, Pakistan, Sri-Lanka, Africa and all. Most of them talk Urdu, Gujarati, languages I never hear about. As soon as they realize I don't speak the language, they cut me off." He swiped a hand near his neck like he was cutting it off. "Plus, to them, we went to Trinidad as laborers, slaves really. We from the lowest class, or caste or whatever, in their—"

"Indian is Indian, Sunil."

"Yeah, Trini-Indians like to think that." He shrugged his shoulders, leaned back in his chair and dropped his plastic fork. "I might look like them, but we not the same. I tell one of them that my mother name Drupatee and he started laughing. He said no one in India would ever name their daughter that. You know how many Trini and Guyanese girls go out with fellas from India, in a serious relationship, thinking they going to get married, only to wake up one morning to find he unfriend them on Facebook and block their number because he back home getting married to the Indian woman his parents pick."

The noisy group was in front of me. They were dragging chairs and tables so they could sit together. I had to raise my voice over the dull sound of wood scraping tile. "Sunil, I have friends. From India. Who come to Trinidad to visit me." I leaned back in my chair too.

"So! You have money. They have money. That is what you have in common. And you are Steven Boodoo daughter." He sounded vexed. "Don't act you don't know that have something to do with it…" He looked at something behind me.

"Sunny!" a voice behind me said.

"Hey," Sunil said when she stood next to our table.

"Padma. My girlfriend, Reshma. Visiting from Trinidad. Reshma. Padma." He pointed at both of us. She put out her hand to shake mine and I took it. "Nice to meet you," I said.

"Same here. Sunny talk about you all the time." She had smooth skin like an airbrushed picture, and she wasn't wearing anything but lipstick. Thick dark hair that had waves like a stale roller set. And the shape? Coke in the bottle, flat belly, small waist, hips and big, big bobbies. A cleavage, like four inches long, was showing at the front of her white T-shirt with the denim jacket over it.

"I ordered during class and just came to pick up, so—" she began.

"You could eat with us if you want." Sunil looked at me for confirmation.

"Yeah, bring your food."

"Okay." She turned to go to the counter. Big round ass in her skinny jeans.

She sat with us and talked while she ate her chicken dumplings. She was from Princes Town just like Sunil. Only people from P-town call him Sunny. (I was wondering about that too, at first.) Said she went to San Fernando Secondary one year behind me. That would make her twenty-three, a year younger than Sunil and me. But she looked younger. Anyway, I didn't remember her. She could have been any one of the groups of girls, a blur of pleated brown skirts and white sneakers, who walked to the taxi stand, rain or shine, while our driver picked us up and Sharma and me argued over whose turn it was to choose a CD to play on the way to lessons.

She was in the same accounting class as Sunil and came to Pot Stickers after her English class every Wednesday. She mentioned Amadou and Nadine a few times, so I guess she was part of the group. I didn't talk on purpose because I wanted her to feel like a third wheel and leave. But Sunil kept asking her questions and looking at me while she spoke, like I was the one who wanted to know the answers. When I couldn't take it anymore, "So, you planning to go home when you finish with your degree?" I asked.

She laughed and her bosom shook, like it was soft and light. "No. I want to stay. It don't have nothing home for me. Where will I get a job? I don't want to work for the public service. My parents don't have connections. Plus, I have smaller brothers and a sister I have to help my parents mind."

"Sunil going back, you know." I hoped my eyes sparkled.

"Yeah. He tell me." She looked at him, put the dirty napkins in the empty dumpling box, and held the box with both hands. "He have business and everything waiting for him when he go back. Sunny just lucky."

"Yes, he is. My lucky man." Sunil had his elbows on the table. I reached across and held one, hoping that he would extend his arm and hold mine. He didn't, so I held on to the fabric of his jacket and rubbed the elbow underneath with one finger.

"You going to college too?" she asked.

"Me?" I laughed. "I have life experience. I running business. Businesses. Since I leave high school. I don't need a business degree." That was a blow she was trying to throw at me. Imagine. "Not like people like you, who don't have business in thcir blood and have to go to school to learn about it."

She moved the box closer to her and moved back in her chair.

I held on to Sunil's other elbow.

She got up. "Well. Nice to meet you, Reshma.

Sunil. See you in class next week, if not before." She smiled, turned, and I watched Sunil follow her out with a shadow across his gray eyes.

When he looked at me, I said, "Country Indian have some big bottom, boy!"

"Resh!" Sunil opened both palms like I was naked and he was trying to cover me, then whispered, "You mustn't say them kinda things."

"But I am a Indian. If I say that about another Indian, how that could be bad? Plus, she ass real big. You sure she not mix?"

"Shhh, Resh." He looked around. The noisy group was leaving so tables and chairs scraped the tile as they were put back.

"Nobody studying we in here. You acting like you never say anything like that. You only here a year and you pick up all them American ways to be touchy about everything. Plus, you didn't hear when she try to insult me first, asking if—"

"We in a public place, Resh. People might get offended. Let we talk about it when we go home, nah. Please." He let out a long breath and his eyes darted around the restaurant, like I was some child misbehaving in public.

I felt like my head was going to explode. "I tired of this effing shit." I got up and went out the door. I walked toward the sound of cars then stopped to read the street signs because nothing looked familiar.

I heard Sunil's voice behind me, calm like none of

it happened. "Not that way. Park is this way. You have your Metrocard ready?"

"Yes," my mouth said against my will.

"Home then."

✌

We were getting dressed to go to the Botanic Gardens. Sunil put on the Zegna jacket over a T-shirt and jeans, and opened the door.

"Where you going?" I was in front the mirror, trying to put my hair in a ponytail.

"To pay the rent. Be right back."

He was gone. The bright day with its car sounds and whistling birds took his place in the doorway. My head throbbed where the black elastic band held it. I took the band out, but the throbbing stayed. I listened between the sounds on Troy Avenue to see if I could hear the exchange between Sunil and the landlady. I thought I was hearing something then a car playing loud music swallowed all the sounds. Barrington Levi's *Living Dangerously* filled up the apartment. It was the remix with Bounty Killah, and Bounty's deep base rounded out Levi's sweetness, warning about all the things that were going to happen to the girl who was living bad. I felt like I wanted to shit and went to the toilet, but nothing happened. I stayed there with the yellow floral dress around my waist and my panties around my ankles until I heard Sunil come back.

"Resh?" he called.

"In here. Coming out now." I got up and flushed.

"You ready?" he asked when I came out. "The pony-tail was looking good."

"Yeah, I ready. I was just thinking the ponytail would be a nice change too." I put my hair up and we left.

"How Mrs. Mannix?" I walked a little behind him along Troy.

"She wasn't home."

I caught up and we held hands. I tried to read the way his hand held mine, how firmly he was holding it, how many fingers were touching me. I studied the pulse in his temple under the skinny gold arm of his aviators. I couldn't read him. He was like a closed fridge. He lifted our hands and touched my cheek with the back of his hand. "Let's take a two-dollar cab to the train station. Okay?"

I nodded, feeling like it was years ago and we were fourteen, going out for the first time. At the corner, he flung out his other arm with a finger pointed, and a dark green Cutlass stopped in front of us.

I had never been to the Botanic Gardens. There was some blossom event going on so the place smelled like one big flower and the gardens were separated according to theme like fragrance, herbs, and things like that. The place was crowded, but not so bad that we couldn't walk or anything. There were mostly old couples who walked and talked slow, and young families that all looked the same in bright-colored expensive clothes that were made to look old, and heavy leather shoes. They all seemed similar with the moms kneeling near their children to teach at every opportunity, and the dads waiting with both hands on the handles of big double strollers.

Sunil went to the bathroom before we left to get lunch at Tom's Restaurant on Washington Avenue. He had left his phone in the bag from the garden's gift shop, and it rang. It was a number from Trinidad so I thought it might be important.

"Hello, this is Sunil phone."

"Hello." His mother had a high-pitched voice.

"Hello, Sunil Mommy."

"Padma?" she asked.

"Mrs. Suinarine, is me—" I was about to say my own name. "Yes, is me, Padma."

"How you? You taking care a Sunny for me?"

"Yes." I put my finger in my other ear to muffle the sounds of the garden.

"How school? You studying hard? Sunny tell me you bright in school."

"Yeah. School going good."

"Good. Good. Where he is? Let me talk to him."

"Oh…He gone out."

"He gone to class?"

"Yeah."

"Okay. Tell him to call me when he come back."

"Yes. I go tell him."

She paused and I heard the TV and people talking

in the background. "He not with she…" she said to someone in the background. "Padma, I—"

I touched the red bar to silence her. Sunil came back just as I ended the call.

"Who call?"

"Your mother."

"I should call she back. Ma don't ever call for nothing." He stepped into the shade to make the call.

"Sunil?"

He looked at me and his eyebrows made a V. "What?" He showed me the phone as in: *Can't you see I'm doing something?*

"How much is your rent?" I had both hands on my hips.

"You know how much it is. You pay it." Lines formed on his forehead.

"I thought you say Mrs. Mannix wasn't home?"

"I thought I could leave my girlfriend in my place and she wouldn't start a CSI investigation?"

"Sunil, you get five thousand a month. You have a set of old clothes. The rent is seven hundred. What you doing with the rest?"

"You and your father want to give me money and tell me how to spend it too? This is some control bullshit. You want receipts? You want pictures of groceries?"

People started to look at us and made big circles as they passed.

"And who really is this Padma? Your"—I made

quotation marks in the air—"'friend.' As you say. Your mother—"

"She is my"—he made quotations too—"'friend.'" And put the phone in his jacket pocket.

"Sunil. On the phone just now, your mother thought I was Padma and ask she if she was taking care of you. Like if Padma is your woman. I look like a ass to you? I know now Padma is the girl who like you to lick she—"

"Lord." He looked around and held me by one elbow. "It have little children here. Let—"

"Don't focking touch me!" I walked away.

Outside the metal gates with the leaf pattern, Eastern Parkway was in front of me. I was sweating so I put the handbag on the ground to take off my jacket, and Sunil picked it up.

"Resh. Calm down. Things not how they look."

"How they look, Sunil? I go tell you. You focking that girl and saving my family money to be with she and stay here. Why else you would be saving money? And your mother and them know about it."

"Resh? You—"

"Let me tell you something. If I find out that you and that girl focking, I will fock she up! Because she getting involved in things that don't concern she. Things that in motion long before she bring she big fat ass around." I wanted to tell him that he was mine. But I didn't want to seem hungry.

"Look. You want to go home?"

"Home? I not going back to that place. I going to the hotel where the walls smooth and the windows not covered with dirt. I was forgetting who I was, Sunil, but I remember now."

A couple was getting out of one of those green taxi-cabs. When they were out, I got in and told the driver I was going to the Soho Grand. I looked back at Sunil, but he was on his phone. Either talking to his mother or whoever. I didn't care. I lay back on the cool seat and tried to think of nothing.

Daddy's friend in the bank said that each month Sunil drew out the money in $500, $500, $500, every day until it's done. The account had $1002.17, just to keep it open and to avoid fees. Daddy wasn't checking the statements, because checking up on Sunil was like checking up on me. I didn't tell Daddy about Padma but, after he told me about the withdrawals, he wanted to know why I wanted to know. "No reason," I said. "Was just wondering."

"You sure everything alright?" Daddy asked.

"Yes. Just wondering." What I was really wondering was if Padma had a bank account. But if I asked that favor, they will call Mr. Boodoo and he might get wise and pull the plug. This was my business and I wanted to handle it. I just had to confirm that he was effing that girl. And I could take it from there. So, the Monday after the gardens, I texted him and asked him to come over so we could talk.

He came right after class and said how he loved me

and that he would never horn me. How I was over-reacting from stress and that Padma was only a friend. When he mentioned her, I gave him a cut eye and he went back to saying he was sorry and how he wanted to marry me when he returned to Trinidad. I smiled a little bit and said that I loved him too. And he started making Indian dance neck movements, while singing "Radhika," this soca chutney love song I hated, but he replaced Radhika's name with mine in the chorus. "Reshma, why you leave and go? Ooooh, Reshma, why you leave and go…" He could be so nice sometimes.

He was doing the usual and I said, "I want to try what you was trying the last time."

"What?" He looked a little scared.

"Eat some." I pointed at the place between my legs.

Apparently, he was really, really, really sorry, because he had to wait till I stopped bucking against the bed, until I came back from a strange new place to the calm beige décor with him in it. Then he cupped my flat ass and turned me over to hit and bite it a few times. Like it was another ass. Kisses covered my body and, when he got to my chest, his eyes were closed. He sighed and seemed far away as he rubbed his face against the plain between my bobbies, like if the space between them was soft and fleshy. When he was inside, he moved in odd patterns, not even hearing the noise my belly was making. He gasped from somewhere deep in his chest, like he never did with me, then fell with his face against my neck. He turned onto his back.

"Hmmm. So that is how Padma like to fock?"

His brow seemed to come down over his eyes, like a lintel on an old house. His nostrils flared. He looked at me like he was trying to think of something to say. "Resh…"

"Don't Resh me. I know, you know. You wasn't focking me. You was focking she. Get up and get out."

He rolled onto his stomach. "I don't know what you talking about. You crazy, oui. I tell you I not—"

"You hear me. Get the fock out!"

He stayed where he was then reached for me with one hand, a smile on his lips. At the same moment, my cell phone rang on the nightstand, a thunderclap in the silent room, and I saw his ass cheeks clench, making an indent at the side and a dimple or two in the smooth pale flesh. I picked up the phone to decline the call, then I got on my knees and started hitting Sunil with the phone. I hit him in the head and started punching him in the back. He got on his knees and held my hands above my head. He kept saying, "Shhh. Shhh. People will come to the room."

I was screaming and only heard myself then. "Get out," I screamed. "Get ouuuuuut!"

"I going, I going…" He put on his pants and shoes, and left with his shirt and knapsack in one hand. After he left, I cried with my head resting on knees I had drawn toward my chest. I couldn't stop. My head felt like it would crack open, and my stomach hurt. Sobs scraping out of my throat were foreign to my ears. It had been a long time. Maybe since my mother died. The shape of Sunil was still on the crisp white sheets. And I thought about what it would be like to live with only the shape of him, and not him, him. Sunil was the only man I was ever with. Since I was fourteen. "Him, him, him…" I shouted to the empty room. Then I lay on the shape that Sunil had left. I remember crying some more, but I don't remember falling asleep.

On Wednesday, I waited across the street from Pot Stickers when I knew her class let out. I waited till she and Nadine came out and I crossed the street just as they turned onto the street from the exit. I wrapped my hand in her hair, yanked her head back, and slapped her across the face. She screamed, turned around, tried to push me then tried to take her hair out of my hands. Her bag of dumplings and her tote bag of books and papers fell on the ground, the papers blowing all over. Nadine tried to push me away with one hand, the food in the other. "This is none of your focking business!" I palmed her face as I said it and she stepped back. Then Miss Padma got brave and started to push me and tried to grab my hair, but it was tied up under my hat, so I bent her head back till she lost her balance and kicked her in the back of the knees, and she fell in a kneeling position. People stopped to look. Some took out their phones. "What the fock you looking at? Don't feel sorry for she. This bitch focking other people man." I went close to her ear. "You know who you focking with?" I slapped her. "Eh cunt, you know?" I did it again. She nodded. "Answer me, yuh muddah cunt!" I pulled her head back, closer to her heels. Her Adam's apple trembled on her exposed neck as she struggled to breathe.

"Yes," she whispered. Tears fell along the sides of her face and made puddles in her ears.

"No! You don't mother cunt know. Because if you did know, you wouldn't be focking my man. You would know to leave him the fock alone. So let me make you wise." I whispered now, "I am Steven Boodoo daughter and if you come near my focking man again, they will just find your cunt dead in New York." I snapped the fingers on one hand. "And we will wipe out your whole clan in Princes Town. You understand?" I hit her in the face and spread the blood on her cheek from where my ring had cut her. "Answer, cunt!"

"Yes." The place where her neck met her head beat like a frightened mouse in a sack of brown skin.

"Now, how much money you and Sunil save?"

She widened her eyes.

"How much?" I punched her in the head.

"Thirty," she croaked. "Thirty thou' sah."

"That is my focking money. Write a check to me for all of it and mail it to Sunil. I know you know where he live. Do it today! You hear me?"

"Yes. My neck."

"Your neck? Your mother cunt!" I let her go. She tried to stand up, one knee on the ground. "This focking girl, playing up in things that don't concern she." I opened my arms and made as if I was going to lunge at her. A small scream escaped her throat. "That is what I thought! Focking cunt!"

Students lined the street in small groups. As I walked past, some lowered their phones and stepped back. When I was clear of them, I hurried to the 6 train on Park.

❧

I was supposed to be in New York for twenty-one days, but I extended it for another four weeks to make all the arrangements. Sunil moved to a nice apartment building near the school, where I could pay the rent with a credit card. And I told Daddy to let me give Sunil his allowance. I cut it to $2500, so he could at least have some cash every month. The day he moved in, I saw Miss Padma by the Jamba Juice. She held her head straight, like she didn't know us. I checked. Sunil didn't even move an eyelash in her direction.

It was the end of June by the time I had to go back. The day before I left, Sunil said he missed home, so I bought a ticket for him and we went back together. In Trinidad, it was just like it was before he left. He stayed with his parents in Princes Town and would sometimes help out in one of the stores then meet me at Club Space in the evenings. On Saturdays we partied till late and did Maracas Beach or Tobago on Sundays. One night at the club, the DJ played this boss soca mix with all my favorite songs, then Sunil got on the mic and asked me to get married. I said yes and there was a party for us afterwards. Sunil bought a small Astor cut diamond in white gold (I get a bigger one in ten years, of course) with the Padma money.

Me. I gave it to him.

Now everything is in order. In August, after Sunil goes back to New York, I will visit him twice a year and he will visit me. And now that we're engaged, when he visits, he could stay at the mansion in Curepe and nobody will bat an eye. When he's done with the business degree and he's up to scratch, we will get married and he will run a store and probably a club in Central Trinidad, because the nightlife seriously dry in Central. I know what you're thinking. But I have that in check too. If Sunil had a feeling of a feeling that he wanted to try something, the doorman to the building is watching everything and will tell me. Plus, three years will go by fast and we will be married, a big wedding with gold threads in my sari. The pictures will take up the whole middle section of the *Trinidad Sunday Guardian*. Now that Sunil and me engaged, and even more so when we get married, any woman he's with will be on the outside. But me, I will always be on the inside.

"I often wonder about winged things in the Caribbean."

– A. K. Herman, always

The Iridescent Blue-Black Boy with Wings (After Márquez)

IT WAS JUST turning light on J'ouvert when Ulysses, covered in dried mud, stumbled up the dirt path toward his grandmother's house. The mud made the shirt collar stand up around his neck, and the pants, tight and torn in places, bunched up at the tops of his thighs. Tired from dancing through the streets of Scarborough since four o'clock that morning, his eyes were half closed, so he could not make out what was moving and whimpering at the side of the track. He had to go up close to see that it was a small, thin boy crouched low to the ground, with one of his wings caught among the barbed shrubs that lined the path.

Confused, Ulysses left the path and ran to wake

Stops. Stops's given name was Lawrence, but he stut-
tered, and the nickname "Starts and Stops" had been
shortened to Stops. The morning had fully arrived,
brilliant and warm, by the time both Stops and Ulysses
stood together staring at the winged thing. Two wings
sprouted from the boy's back. The child's body and his
wings were covered with short, iridescent, blue-black
hair, so he shimmered in the new day. Each of the
boy's arms ended in a three-fingered hand with black
nails. Besides wings, there were buds of horns, black
and spiraling outward, on either side of his head. The
eyes, black too, stared from a face with an upturned
mouse-like nose and a human mouth that exposed
sharp white teeth whenever the boy grimaced.

"It dey li-like a bat. Bu-but in hu-human form,"
said the stouter of the two.

"Yuh tink we should help it?" Ulysses was thin and
as tall as a door.

Stops poked it with a stick. The boy whimpered
and tried to cover himself with his free wing.

"Ye-yeah."

"You go roun' de odder side and leh go de wing."
The trapped wing was freed and folded next to its coun-
terpart, and still the boy did not move. Stops squatted
in front of the child and offered one end of Ulysses's
mud-caked shirt, then reversed a little. He did this
a few times until the child got the hint, grasped the
shirt, and followed Stops to Ulysses's grandmother's
house. The house was built on an incline, so it rested

on short concrete piles at the back and on long ones at the front. The two friends locked the boy and the muddy shirt in an old chicken coop at the narrowest space under the house.

❧

Ulysses's grandmother, Miss Pauline, lived in one of over a dozen houses scattered on a long brush- and tree-covered hill, called First Hill, which leveled to a plateau at the top. The plateau was called "the flat." Most people in Hillsborough Village lived on a slope or on a flat. At the base of First Hill was Windward Road, the main road that connected the village to the rest of Tobago. Next to the road were clusters of shrubs and small trees, then a craggy drop to Hillsborough Bay below. The rhythm of waves hitting rocks ordered all life in the village, the very breath of its people, though those who lived there ceased to hear it soon after they were born. Among the houses on the slope lived Miss Vic, Stops's great aunt who had reared him since his mother left to go to the shop at the base of First Hill and never returned. There were the Millers, who argued with each other from early morning till late at night. Mr. Miller took to his bed some years ago and refused to work. He and Eta Miller had four sons and three daughters. Stops and Ulysses were friends with the eldest boy, Michael. Carla was Michael's best friend. She lived on the flat but spent most of her time at the Millers's or with Miss Vic.

On Mardi Gras, Ulysses, Stops, Michael, Carla, and most of the people of First Hill went to see the parade in town. Ulysses had forgotten about the captive until later that day some of the neighbors' dogs circled the house, barking and snarling but never venturing under the house. That night, the two friends told their secret to Michael and Carla, and the four moved the creature to an abandoned latrine behind a stand of trees further up the hill, almost to the flat. Once the creature was in the latrine, the four friends made a pact to not speak their full names where the child might hear and to not tell anyone about it. At first, they took care to heed the terms of the pact, but as time passed, they forgot.

❧

"Mi swear mi nuh tell nobody," Carla protested.

"Mi nuh tell nobody needer." Michael shrugged, staring at the young man who had bound up the hill, intent on seeing an iridescent blue-black boy with wings. Like some, the visitor covered his mouth and ran down the hill, not really believing what he saw. Others sucked their teeth and cursed, annoyed that Ulysses and Stops would dress a small child as a bat and lock it in a latrine to fool people. Once the secret was out, Ulysses convinced two girls from Hope Village to give him a feel in exchange for a look. Stops tried the same, but allowed the girl to see the child before he could secure the illicit stroke. Most days after school, the four friends gathered at the place outside the latrine, which was now clear of underbrush and furnished with discarded crates and large biscuit tins arranged in a circle. Here they ate and played cards, entertaining visitors to the latrine until late at night.

≪⑤

In the many weeks since J'ouvert, no one bothered to feed the child. When Ulysses looked in to see why no squeaking or fluttering was coming from the latrine, the flashlight showed an emaciated boy with sores on his knees and torn paper-like wings. Carla opened the door and threw in mangoes and Dominican figs. The child, his back pressed against the gray-black wooden walls, nibbled at the fruit. From that day, he was fed occasionally with fruit and leftovers. The child never grew fat, but the wings began to heal and the blue-black hair shone almost as brilliantly as it did that J'ouvert.

≪⑤

People came from as far as Charlotteville and Speyside to see the winged boy. Some came during the night, and, one April evening after school, the four friends arrived to find the latrine flanked by two bamboo poles that flew bright-colored cotton flags marked with convoluted symbols. At the base of the flags were enamel basins heaving with fried and stewed meats, raisin rice, macaroni pie, fruit cake, sponge cake, sugar cake, and bottles of white rum.

~

"Wha mas' yuh playin' nex' year, Carls, mud or oil?" Ulysses picked a card from the pile on the crate.

"Wha' everybody else playin'." She fanned away the flies and summer heat with her free hand.

"Mi a play pan wid Hope Pan Groovers fuh de J'ouvert— " Selwyn began.

"Yuh cyan do de two. Is mas or pan." Michael's ankle hit the tin he was sitting on and made a hollow metal sound.

The friends, now five, since Carla's boyfriend, Selwyn, went everywhere with them, grew silent and pretended to concentrate on their rummy hands. A cool breeze from the bay whistled up the hill, nodding the leaves of a thin Hog Plum tree that grew next to the latrine. For a moment, four of them almost heard the waves crashing against the rocks again. The winged child felt the breeze too, and a clumsy flap came from the latrine as he tried to catch the air in his taut, smooth wings.

"Ah we ah pl-pl-play d-devil mas. Nex' year."

"Mi go like fi see yuh as a devil." Selwyn grinned and hugged Carla.

Carla, a plump, bottle-skinned beauty, lazed in Selwyn's embrace, wondering if it would be a mistake to end the relationship with the funny, good-natured butcher's son from Hope Village and claim the kind but brooding Michael she had always loved. She was wondering if Miss Vic might have some advice when Ulysses poked her in the side.

"Yeah, Carls, ah we go need soot from yuh muma fireside. We go be real devils. Like long time."

"Y-yeah. W-wid h-h-horns. An ch-ch-chains."

"Mi daddy cyan get real sheep horn an' ting from de abattoir," Selwyn ventured.

"Real ting? We want four pair?" Carla moved her cards around.

"Four easy fi get." Selwyn stroked his chin and winked at Carla.

"Carls, nuh forget fi scrape de soot from de pot-dem," Ulysses added.

"Mi go collect, but if Ma find out, she go say mi studyin' Ca'nival and not O-levels. Every day she ah sey how August almost finish an—"

"Yeah. Miss Pauline on mi case 'bout exams too."

"M-Miss Vic s-say sh-she w-want see fi—"

"Five subjects!" Carla, Selwyn, and Ulysses finished the sentence.

"Leh de man finish he sentence, nah," Michael chided and sucked his teeth.

"F-five s-s-subjects." Stops lowered his cards and Ulysses peered at the disjointed hand of spades and aces.

"Yeah. Maybe we should hang less. Study more and plan Ca'nival on de side." Ulysses was looking for a six of hearts. The six came down when it was Selwyn's turn and Carla's boyfriend picked it up. Ulysses turned his hopes toward a ten of hearts.

"Yeah. Might 'ave fi come less to de Hill too." Selwyn winked at Carla. "And, gin," he added absently, put down his cards and stood to stretch his tall, muscular form. "Time to go, Carla, babes. Walk me to de road?"

The game finished. Michael stared into his losing hand, taking only a fleeting glance at Carla as she left with Selwyn. To Carla, it seemed that Michael had grown gruff and distant, barely ever looking at her. He regarded her this way because he loved her with such magnitude that he could no longer take in the sight of her whole person and had resolved to love her piecemeal. On the night of Carla and Selwyn's wedding, Michael would climb onto the Millers's roof and sob with both hands over his mouth. He would leave Tobago for Trinidad never having told her how he felt, but made up for it by marrying a girl from San Fernando who was plump and bottle-skinned.

❧

It was early evening, and the blinking holiday lights from the houses cast an eerie, staccato glow among the trees and shrubs, and a thin fog hung in the air, blurring forms on First Hill. From where they stood in the concrete gallery, Miss Pauline and Miss Vic could not see the St. George's Christian Soldiers stationed at the base of the hill. The church group had stopped singing Christmas hymns and sent up the junior pastor, Brother Bernard Campbell, a handsome, charismatic young man for whom the church was raising money to send to the seminary at Oxford. At Oxford, Bernard would fall in love with an English woman and became a doctor. He would never return to Tobago and never return the church's money.

Bernard seemed to materialize at the base of the steps that led to the gallery.

"Oh, is Likkle Pastor," Miss Pauline called out. She was dressed in a pale-blue organdy dress, opaque stockings, and white plastic house slippers.

"Whey de res' a de delegation?" Miss Vic asked. She was also in Sunday clothes, and red marabou-trimmed house slippers.

Bernard took the steps two by two. At the top of the stairs there was no railing, only the fog, the night sky and, in the distance, the white frothy tips of waves hitting the rocks in the bay. For a moment he stood alone at the top of the world and was giddy. His unsteady feeling ended when he wiped his feet on the coconut fiber mat, and folded himself into the ornate wrought-iron chair he was offered. The chair pressed its curly shapes into his back and cut off the circulation in one of his legs.

"Um…some a dem don' want to come up—" Bernard began.

"De track too muddy?" Miss Pauline interrupted. "Mi granson trow sand on it jus' dis marnin'. Mi could get 'im fi help Sister Graham an' Brother Cecil up de hill."

Bernard's eyes were grim and his jaw fixed. "Is not de mud—"

"What den?" Miss Vic asked.

Bernard explained there were rumors that Ulysses housed and fed a devil on the hill. The children, nieces, and nephews of many church members corroborated the story. Even the pastor's daughter, who had died for a few minutes and had had a vision of angels, said Ulysses was in league with Lucifer. The delegation could not come up the hill until they were sure the rumor was not true.

Before Miss Pauline could answer, Miss Vic stood in front of Bernard with her hands on her hips. In her Christmas red dress and matching marabou-trimmed slippers, she was an ibis about to pluck something off of his head.

"If de devil de pan dis hill, Pastor, wid de power he 'ave," she paused then shouted, "de power vested in 'im will know. Pastor feelin' de presence a evil?" Her voice tried to escape the concrete porch but dissolved in the damp night air.

"Well...mi don' know, Miss Vic."

"Well, go an ask 'im."

Pastor could not say that he felt the presence of evil. The elders of the church, impaired by desire for Miss Pauline's fruit cake, closed their eyes and placed their hands on their chests and reported that the Deceiver was nowhere to be found. On his third trip up the hill, Little Pastor was at the rear of the delegation, supporting Sister Graham, who at that moment decided to use the big village susu hand that was coming to her to help fund Bernard's theological education at Oxford.

The last of the prayer group left close to midnight. When Miss Pauline and Miss Vic had passed the stand of trees farther up the hill, almost to the flat, they found that the rains, in full gear since September, had thickened the grass, muddied the ground, and raised the level of underground filth such that every other breath of the wind carried a fecal odor. The air at the circle of crates and tins was thick with mosquitoes that bred in the uncovered pit of the latrine and irritated everyone on the hill. The two women crossed the grassy threshold and held their kerosene lamps up to the dilapidated privy. Miss Pauline fumbled with the wooden latch, not really believing the tale of her church members. Victorine placed her hand over Pauline's and mouthed the word *no*. Under a sudden light rain, they backed away from the latrine so Miss Vic could throw a stone against the door. The powdery thud was answered by a faint flutter at which Vic leaned her head and looked at her friend as if to ask, *You see?* The sound had startled the iridescent blue-black boy, who perched on the wooden seat, ate mosquitoes, avoided the water dripping through the roof, and grew.

∽

Miss Pauline was not as angry as Ulysses thought she would be. She did not wake to see him off to school for a few days and as she did her housework, she muttered something about a daughter who had started another family in Trinidad and never looked back. One evening when she had reached the limits of her vexation, Miss Pauline interrupted Ulysses while he was studying with Stops and asked that he and his friends clean up around the latrine for the holiday season. Together, the four friends trimmed the grass and stripped the latrine of its pennants, leaving only the offerings of food out of fear that they were part of some fiendish contrivance between a supplicant and their winged captive. The food had turned to a black glue-like mass that stuck to the enamel basins, and the rains had washed the labels from the bottles of rum. On Boxing Day, before anyone else awoke, Miss Pauline, with a broom made of stripped coconut fronds, swept the alcohol and stained utensils into a large plastic bag. She reasoned that not even the devil would want such food.

෫

On the Saturday before J'ouvert, moonlight white-washed the dried grass and the tree leaves so Stops could easily discern his way along the parched, pot-holed earth to the latrine. He walked slowly, trying not to perspire in the hot, dry air. The armpits of his dress shirt were soon wet, so he put down the bag of leftover food, took off the shirt, and marched on in cotton vest and slacks. When he got to the circle of crates and tins, the latrine was shaking. The captive inside squealed as it banged against the walls. Stops could not decide whether to hold the latrine still to stop it from breaking apart or to run to his friends, who were at the base of the hill waiting to catch a taxi to Scarborough. He did the latter.

"Wha' we go do?" Carla asked, worried that Selwyn was waiting by himself outside Club Bluefly. Each time the walls of the latrine shook, they took one step back.

"Open it?" Ulysses asked. "It soundin' big. When was de las' time anybody see it?"

Michael strode forward, opened the door, and scampered away.

The latrine got still.

With his head down, the winged blue-black boy stumbled from the latrine, crunching the dried grass as he went. The wings were folded like tents on his back and each blue-black hair seemed tipped in silver as it caught the moonlight. When the boy raised his head, his horns, obsidian black, were as long and as thick as a child's arm and spiraled to two glassy points. He stopped, jet-colored eyes staring, and seemed to regard his captors. A rush of stale air hit the four in their faces as the boy's wings extended to their full span, at least five feet each, then folded again. Stops broke the ranks and held out the bag of food. The boy, now almost as tall as Ulysses, took the bag, leaned his head expectantly to one side, and filled his mouth with rice and chicken bones. After a few handfuls, he turned the bag inside out and, finding it empty, dropped it. He flapped his wings a few times to lift a few inches off the ground. Finally, he sat atop a wooden crate, folded his wings, and scratched his belly.

෪

Ulysses was still mixing the soot with lard when the dark form flew from the latrine roof, disappearing into the darkness above. It was just before three o' clock on J'ouvert. Carla, dressed in shorts and a tattered T-shirt, was helping Stops attach his sheep horns. The horns, smooth and gray, still had the bitter, acrid odor of singed hair and flesh. Michael, in horns and a length of chain around his waist, danced and admired his rotund shadow in the light of the kerosene lamp. When the lard mixture was ready, the four smeared themselves all over till they were a gleaming blackest black. With cords tied around their chests and waists, they attached burlap wings blackened with paint. Ulysses carried a heavy glass bottle filled with water and a metal spoon. Carla gave everyone a whistle before they extinguished the lamps and made their way carefully down the hill to the main road, every now and then glancing up at the indigo sky.

The four friends met the J'ouvert procession on Windward Road, at John Dial Village, going toward Scarborough. The procession was made up of revelers from most of the lowland villages—Hope, Mount St. George, Goodwood, Pembroke. Hope Pan Groovers Steel Orchestra, racked like cutlery on a Bedford truck, led the way, playing the year's calypso hits. Sometimes Carla caught a glimpse of Selwyn playing the nine bass and shadow-danced with him. Each time her hips churned, he laughed and hit the bass harder. To support the steel band, revelers' voices were layered on whistles blown in unison. The shrill call of the whistles rubbed up against the crystalline clatter of glass bottles struck with spoons and tire rims played with lengths of iron. Housewives, husbands, teachers, doctors, lawyers, and children were baptized in mud, paint, crude oil, and soot to become the revelers that make up the J'ouvert. Red, black, and blue vampire bats shook their fabric wings in time with the steel band music. Jab Molassie writhed on the paved streets, drinking from enameled chamber pots. A family of shredded burlap gorillas scratched and sniffed each other. Ulysses's band from last year, mischievous teens covered in Hope River mud, filled the middle of the procession. And devils of all colors dragged chains and carried pitchforks and empty tins to force onlookers in Scarborough to pay de devil or be smeared with soot, paint, mud, worse.

Just before dawn, the village bands merged in town, peopling the capital with strange folk. Sometimes two steel band trucks ended up next to each other and their music had an altercation in the space between them. Onlookers pointed, danced, and avoided mud-covered masqueraders who searched the crowd, hoping to rub their corrupt skins onto their well-dressed friends.

Here and there the street lamps revealed families of

winged devils. But when the four friends went to have a closer look, they discovered the cords that held the beings together. It was Stops who saw a shadow plummet out of the sky into the old market, just behind a crowd of spectators. He darted in its direction. Ulysses followed him. They both halted at a swath of shadow just beyond the streetlights. Beneath the music, Stops and Ulysses could make out the familiar sound of wings rubbing against each other. When the young men squinted, the light settled in places, revealing an assembly of shimmering blue-black persons with thick spiraling horns and wings folded on their backs. Stops placed one foot within the streetlight's glow and the iridescent contours turned their attention on him and his friend. When the friends took another step, the gleaming, iridescent outlines retreated, and a determined wind pelted the dried earth, its famished grass, and paper wrappers into their faces. Shielding their eyes from the debris, Ulysses and Stops ran toward the winged beings, only to end up under a bright morning, behind a group of people taking a break from the parade.

"Yuh see dat?" Ulysses asked a stout man who, from the neck down, was a gorilla with blackened, shredded burlap fur. The gorilla's head lay on the ground, eyeless and unable to look at the sky.

"See wha? Is ca' nival. Plenty fi see."

"A big crowd…blue devils? Passin' right here?"

"See plenty devil today. Devil all over town."

"You nuh feel a heavy breeze?"

"Dat was jus' a rude sea breeze coming off de harbor to dance wid ah we." He took up his head and went back to the parade.

Stops and Ulysses were staring up at the sky, so clear it was like a blue bed sheet had been thrown over the world, when Carla and Michael found them.

"It gone?" Michael asked, looking up at the sky.

"He gone ent?" Carla turned her gaze upward.

They surveyed the sky till their eyes stung. Then, one by one, each of them adjusted their horns, tightened the cords that secured their wings, and danced back to the parade.

Acknowledgments

Thank you, Almighty God, for the gift of writing, creativity, light, music, mercy, truth, and love. Thank you, Saints, for who you are and all you do. Auldith and Lynette, your stories inspire me to tell stories of my own. Thanks, Jugs and Mame, for all your encouragement and for the hours and hours of conversation about the way people lived in the past. Bongo and Ikbal, thanks for endless discussions on plot, characters and for reading drafts. Moy, April, and Eli, thanks for listening. Geeta, you helped me turn a corner on this journey and I'll be ever grateful to you for it. Mubanga, thanks for championing my writing and for your mentorship. Thanks to the editors of all the literary journals who published my stories. *Lolwe* and *Doek*! thanks for making me part of your community. To the people, places and languages of the Caribbean, especially my beloved Tobago and her sister Trinidad, this is all inspired by you. Thank you for your complexity, for not making sense all the time, for inventing new art forms, and for inviting artists of all kinds to play for the sake of playing. I play for you.

About the Author

A. K. Herman is a poet and fiction writer, born in Scarborough, Tobago. She has published poems and short stories in several online and print publications, including *Doek! Literary Journal, Lolwe*, the *Waterstone Review* and *Shenandoah*. She has been shortlisted for the Commonwealth Short Story Prize. *The Believers: Stories* is her debut collection. A. K. lives in New York.

Printed in the USA
CPSIA information can be obtained
at www.ICGtesting.com
JSHW020709161124
73674JS00005B/15

9 781948 788014

Printed in the USA
CPSIA information can be obtained
at www.ICGtesting.com
JSHW020709161124
73674JS00005B/15

9 781948 788014